trouble don't last

trouble don't last

shelley pearsall

A Dell Yearling Book

Published by
Dell Yearling
an imprint of
Random House Children's Books
a division of Random House, Inc.
New York

Visit us on the Web! www.randomhouse.com/kids

Educators and librarians, for a variety of teaching tools, visit us at
www.randomhouse.com/teachers

ISBN: 0-440-41811-9

Reprinted by arrangement with Alfred A. Knopf

Printed in the United States of America

December 2003

10 9 8 7 6

OPM

For my family
who always believed

CONTENTS

Keep your eye on the sun
See how she run.
Don't let her catch you with your work undone.
I'm a trouble, I'm a trouble.
Trouble don't last always.

—Virginia slave song

trouble don't last

Trouble

Truth is, trouble follows me like a shadow.

To begin with, I was born a slave when other folks is born white. My momma was a slave and her momma a slave before that, so you can see we are nothing but a family of trouble. Master sold Momma before I was even old enough to remember her, and two old slaves named Harrison and Lilly had to raise me up like I was one of their own, even though I wasn't. Then, when I was in my eleventh year, the old slave Harrison decided to jump into trouble himself, and he tried to run away.

Problem was, I had to go with him.

The Broken Plate

It all started on a just-so day in the month of September 1859, when I broke my master's plate while clearing the supper table. I tried to tell Lilly that if Master Hackler hadn't taken a piece of bread and sopped pork fat all over his old plate, I wouldn't have dropped it.

But Lilly kept her lips pressed tight together, saying nothing as she scraped the vegetable scraps into the hog pails.

"And Young Mas Seth was sticking his foot this-away and that-away, tryin to trip me up," I added.

Lilly didn't even look at me, just kept scraping and scraping with her big, brown hands.

"Maybe it was a spirit—could be Old Mas Hackler's dead spirit—that got ahold of me right then and made that plate fly right outta my hands."

Lilly looked up and snorted, "Spirits. If Old Mas Hackler wanted to haunt this house, he'd go an' turn a whole table on its end, not bother with one little china plate in your hands." She pointed her scraping knife at me. "You gotta be more careful, Samuel, or they gonna sell you off sure as anything, and I can't do nothin to help you then. You understand me, child?"

"Yes'm," I answered, looking down at my feet. Every time Lilly said something like this to me, which was more often than not, it always brought up the same picture in my head. A picture of my momma. She had been sold when I was hardly even standing on my own two legs. Right after the Old Master Hackler had died. Lilly said that selling off my momma paid for his fancy carved headstone and oak burying box, but I'm not sure all that is true.

In my mind, I could see my momma being taken away in the back of Master's wagon, just the way Lilly told me. Her name was Hannah, and she was a tall, straight-backed woman with gingerbread skin like mine. Lilly said that she was wearing a blue-striped headwrap tied around her hair, and she was leaning over with her head down in her hands when they rode off. The only thing Lilly knew was that they took her to the courthouse in Washington, Kentucky, to sell her.

After my momma had gone, it had fallen on Lilly's shoulders to raise me as if I was her own boy, even though she wasn't any relation of mine and she'd already had two sons and four daughters, all sold off or dead. But she said I had more trouble in me than all six of her children rolled up together. "I gotta be on your heels day and night," she was always telling me. "And even that don't keep the bad things from happening."

When she was finished with the hog pails, Lilly came over to me. "How's that chin doin?" She lifted the cold rag I'd been holding and looked underneath. "Miz Catherine got good aim, I give her that."

After I had broken the china plate, Master Hackler's loud, redheaded wife, Miz Catherine, had flung her table fork at me.

"You aren't worth the price of a broken plate, you know that?" she hollered, and sent one of the silver forks flying. Good thing I had sense enough not to duck my head down, so it hit right where she was aiming, square on my chin. Even though it stung all the way up to my ear, I didn't make a face. I was half-proud of myself for that.

"You pick up every little piece," Miz Catherine had snapped, pointing at the floor. "Every single piece with those worthless, black fingers of yours, and I'll decide what to do about your carelessness."

After that, Lilly had come barreling in to save me. She had helped me sweep up the white shards that had flown all over, and she told Miz Catherine that she would pay for the plate. Master usually gave Lilly a dollar to keep every Christmas. "What you think that plate cost?" Lilly asked Miz Catherine as she swept.

"How much do you have?" Miz Catherine sniffed.

"Maybe $4 saved up."

"Then I imagine it will cost you $4."

So the redheaded devil Miz Catherine had taken most of Lilly's savings just for my broken plate—although, truth was, Lilly really had $6 tucked away. And she had given me a banged-up chin. But, as Lilly always said, it could have been worse.

Then we heard Master Hackler's heavy footsteps coming down the hall. He walks hard on his heels, so you can always tell him from the others.

"You be quiet as a country graveyard," Lilly warned. "And

gimme that cloth." Quick as anything, she snatched the cloth from my chin and began wiping a plate with it.

"Still cleaning up from supper?" Master Hackler said, peering around the doorway. "Samuel's made you mighty slow this evening, Lilly."

"Yes, he sho' has." Lilly kept her head down and wiped the plates in fast circles. "But I always git everything done, you know. Don't sleep a wink till everything gits done."

"What should we do about the boy's carelessness, Lilly?" he asked in a hard voice. I could feel my throat tighten, as if a big snake had wrapped itself around it.

"Samuel's nothin but a child," Lilly answered, calm and even-voiced as always. "Still learning how to keep ahold of his self."

"Catherine thinks he ought to be punished, so he's more careful next time. A few stripes of cowhide would make a difference, she says."

The snake squeezed tighter, and I dug my fingers into my palms.

"I always git after him for his carelessness, Mas Hackler. You know I does," Lilly continued, laying on her sweet tone smooth as jam on a slice of bread. "I'm gonna take away his supper tonight. I got a good bean soup and a peach pie made, and I ain't giving him even a bite. Goin hungry, that's what gits to a boy his age."

Master walked to the corner of the kitchen where I slept.

"Going cold ought to get to him too." I could hear him snatch up my two blankets. "I'll take these for tonight, maybe tomorrow night. You see to it, Lilly, that he doesn't curl up on those hearth-stones to keep warm."

"Yessir, I will. You can be sho' I will."

Master's big shadow stood over me. "You're as weak and chickenhearted as a girl," he spat. "Got to have some old, slave woman stand up and fight for you." And then the heels pounded away from me, and took the snake around my throat with them.

Once Master Hackler was out of earshot, Lilly said sharply, "Git up and open that kitchen door, Samuel." She hefted up the tub of old dishwater and carried it outside. While I stood there, Lilly flung the water hard as she could into Master's yard. It splattered like an angry rain over the steps, the yard, and the few scraggly plants in the kitchen garden.

"You mad at Mas Hackler?" I asked. "For what he said?"

Lilly turned and glared at me with eyes that had changed to smoldering coals in her dark face. "No. But I sho' is mad at you. You always go and bring me troubles I don't need." She slammed the tin tub down on the step. "I'm old and I seen enough hard times in my life. Now, you go on and take them hog scraps to Harrison in the barn 'cause I don't even wanta look at you any-more this evening."

I could feel the hot tears coming into my eyes. Lilly said folks were only allowed to cry if people were near dying or dead,

6

so I tried to keep her from seeing my eyes filling up faster than a pump at a trough.

Keeping my head down, I grabbed the hog pails from the kitchen. But Lilly's hand latched onto my arm as I hurried through the door. I thought she was going to give me one of her talking-to's.

Instead, she said in a low voice, "You ask Harrison for something to eat, you hear? I promised Master that I wouldn't give you no food, but I didn't promise him no one else would." She gave me a little push.

"Now, git outta my sight."

Harrison's Warning

I found Harrison in the barn greasing Master Hackler's riding boots. Harrison was the oldest person on Master's farm. He didn't even know his true age, but he said he figured he was close to threescore and ten, give or take a handful of years.

I pulled up a milking stool and watched him rub circles of sharp-smelling bootblack into the leather. His fingers were so stiff from being old that they always reminded me of wood spindles, and I could hardly keep my eyes from staring at them and thinking about all my fingers turning into pieces of wood someday.

"Mas'er Hackler told me his boots been leakin'," Harrison said slowly, without looking up. "So I'm a-gonna make them good and black." He spit on the boot top to make the grease smooth. "Need bootblack on them fancy leather boots of yours, Samuel?" Even though he was looking down, I could see a slow grin wrinkling across his face.

"I ain't got boots," I said. With my shirtsleeve, I took a quick swipe at drying my eyes. "I ain't even got a pair of shoes to wear 'til November."

"Well, how you gonna keep yo' tender, brown feet dry, then?" Harrison slapped his leg and laughed so hard that I could see all his missing teeth, which were a lot. I laughed too, even though I wasn't sure what he thought was so downright funny.

Then Harrison grew serious and gave me a look. "So I hear

you got yo'self in trouble with Mas'er and Miz Catherine again. That true?"

I studied the hog scraps in the pails—browning apple cores, turnip greens, red tops of beets, all mixed together. *Hogs could eat food right off whitefolks' plates,* I thought, *and not have to worry about a thing.*

"Broke a good plate and put Miz Catherine in a fit. That why you crying them big ol' tears?" Harrison looked up. "You gonna answer me sometime 'fore the day of the Great, Samuel?" he said sharply.

I didn't say a word.

Heaving a loud sigh, Harrison set the riding boot down and stood up. "Think you got hard times, huh? You ain't seen no hard times yet, Samuel. Mine and Lilly's hard times is almost over, but your hard times is all ahead of you."

I could tell what Harrison was doing next. He was turning around and lifting up his shirt back so I could look at them. I had seen them a hundred times, and seeing them always brought the snake twisting back around my throat.

"You look right here, son. Look at what I'm showin you."

I couldn't do a thing but look up at them again. On Harrison's stooped brown back, the terrible stripes tore back and forth like the jagged scars that lightning makes when it splits through the bark of trees. Seeing them made me feel weak all over and sick.

"Them's hard times, child. You just remember that," he

said softly, letting his shirt slide back down. Then, turning back toward me, Harrison put his arm around my shoulders and gave them a hard squeeze.

" 'Nough that," he said. "You know what I'm sayin to you. Now, let's git them hogs fed 'fore they start chewin up the walls of the barn."

Outside, Master kept a couple of big sows and some smaller hogs. I called the fattest, red-backed one Miz Catherine, when no one was around, and an ugly runt with a two-color nose was Young Mas Seth.

It would be slaughtering time come December, and Master said he wanted them all getting nice and fat. Young Mas Seth was already plump and Miz Catherine, she filled up half a barn door. The real ones and the hog ones both.

I helped Harrison heave the pails into the hogs' trough, and we watched them squeal and fight their way into the slop. It reminded me again that Lilly had made a peach pie, and that I wasn't supposed to get a thing to eat that night unless Harrison gave me something. But, truth was, I knew Lilly'd try to pinch and save some for me to eat the next morning, if I kept quiet about it.

As we leaned over the fence watching the hogs, Harrison cleared his throat loudly and said, "Sleep with your top eye open this evenin, you hear me, Samuel?"

"What?"

Harrison stared up at the dark windows of the house for a minute, as if someone's eyes might be watching us. "I says, keep a look out this evenin," he repeated, under his breath. "Things is gonna happen then, I hear."

"What?" I could feel my heart thud in my chest. "Is something happenin to me?"

"Might be."

"What's gonna happen?"

"Can't say. Just look out. That's all I'm tellin you."

Right then, Master's oldest son, Cassius, came flying out of the house. He was trying to pull on his black frock coat, with one sleeve stuck out the wrong direction. I figured he was probably going to take one of Master Hackler's horses down the road to the Eagle Tavern in Blue Ash, Kentucky, where he would drink rum and carry on for half the night. And his hat was already setting the wrong way on his head, I could tell.

"I gotta saddle a horse for that one," Harrison said, pulling a thumb toward Cassius. "You just look out, like I tol' you."

Cassius had almost reached the edge of the yard.

"You sayin look for something good or bad?" I tried to ask while Harrison was moving away.

"Just look, that's all." Harrison flung a stray turnip into the hog pen. "Go on now, child." He flapped his hand at me. "Go."

"Tell me," I kept on, my voice rising. "They sellin someone off? That what you heard?"

11

"Git away from me 'fore you git me in a heap a' trouble," Harrison hissed. "You do the things you s'posed to be doin. I got my own work to do."

So I couldn't do a thing but watch his hunched-over back disappear into the shadowy darkness of the stalls, knowing that something was about to happen to us.

Old Master Hackler's Ghost

The kitchen was cold and silent as death that night. Even the mice that usually scratched and scuttled along the shelves weren't making any sounds.

Sleep with your top eye open, Harrison had said.

And before going to her cabin for the night, Lilly had warned me to stay away from the warm hearthstones, like Master had ordered.

So I huddled on my straw tick, staring at the embers glowing in the black belly of the fireplace far across the room. Although I wanted to crawl over and warm myself by the fire, I didn't dare move. Maybe someone had his eyes on me, maybe that's what Harrison had meant.

I looked up and wondered if Master Hackler could see between the wide beams of the kitchen ceiling. His bedchamber was right up there. Perhaps one of his gray eyes was peering down at me, at that very moment, waiting for me to creep toward the hearth, where it was warm. Then he'd come pounding downstairs, cowhide me, and take me to the courthouse in Washington, Kentucky, to sell me, same as my poor momma.

It was too quiet in the house. Most times when I slept in the kitchen I could hear the fire popping, or the loose shutter upstairs creaking back and forth. Or Master Hackler's loud snoring and Miz Catherine's whistling noises. Seemed like the whole house was holding its breath. I closed my eyes and tried to think of something else besides being hungry for Lilly's bean soup and peach pie, and being as shivery as I'd ever been.

My mind started wandering to the Old Master Hackler, who had died in the bedchamber upstairs years before. He was one of the meanest, sorriest men that God ever put breath in or took breath out of. That's what Lilly said.

Harrison had seen his ghost more than a few times near the barn, and he told me Old Master Hackler was still wearing the same black cloth suit he was buried with. Only his ghost didn't have any skin.

The thought of the rattling skeleton of Old Master Hackler walking around in his burial suit prickled all the skin on my arms and legs.

That's when I heard a noise outside the kitchen.

It was the scraping sound of the kitchen door slowly creaking open and a draft of cold night air gliding through. Closing my eyes, I slid myself back into the shadows of the kitchen corner. Soft footsteps shuffled through the doorway. The footsteps moved toward the dining room, stopped, and turned back toward the kitchen. Slowly, they crossed the kitchen floor, looking for something.

I pulled in my breath as they moved past the cupboards and over to the stone hearth. Coming closer. Then they slid quickly toward the corner where I was hiding. Before I could move, an old hand smelling of dust and earth reached down from above and clamped itself across my mouth.

Old Master Hackler had come for me!

In the darkness, I thrashed my arms back and forth and tried to call out for Master and Miz Catherine, so they would know a dead man's spirit was stealing me away to the grassy burying-ground. But, even dead, Old Master Hackler was as strong as an ox. He held my mouth tight-shut and twisted a bony arm around me.

Keep your top eye open, Harrison had warned.

Maybe Harrison had known that Old Master Hackler's ghost was abroad that night. Maybe he had known his dead spirit would be trying to whisk people's souls away.

Although I felt like dying of fright, I opened one eye and stared straight up at the ghost, thinking that would scare it off. Maybe that's what Harrison had been trying to tell me. Keep your top eye open.

But instead of seeing the skeleton face of Old Master Hackler grinning in front of me, I found myself looking right into the wild eyes of Harrison himself.

"Be quiet, child," he whispered, holding my mouth so hard I could taste the dust on his hands. "Lord Almighty, just hush up."

Around us, the house was suddenly filled with sound. Upstairs, Master Hackler started coughing loudly, and the slop jar scraped across the floor. Then the back door slammed. Cassius came cursing and stumbling into the hall, returning from his card playing.

Harrison's hand tightened, and I could feel his whole arm begin to tremble.

But Cassius didn't walk toward all the commotion we were making in the kitchen. He started up the hall stairs instead. We could hear him talking and humming to himself like a person gone mad, and he missed the last step on the stairs, same as always. There was the loud smack of his knees hitting the top floor, a sharp curse, and then a shuffling sound as he crawled toward his room, feeling nothing on account of too much rum, of course.

Right after that, two barn cats started up an unearthly yowling outside, and a gust of wind made the shutter upstairs start banging.

As I waited there in the darkness, my mind was spinning with questions. Why had Harrison crept into the kitchen to get me? Was someone coming after him? Or me? Had Lilly taken sick? Had something gone wrong in the barn?

But Harrison kept his hand over my mouth, and stayed as still as if he'd turned to stone. I couldn't speak a word, or even hardly breathe.

"Ain't nothin wrong, Samuel," he whispered finally. "You just listen to me now. Ain't nothin wrong," and I could feel his hand loosening little by little.

"Why you here?" I asked as soon as I was allowed enough room to speak, but Harrison didn't answer. He stood up and tugged on my arm to get me up. That's when I noticed that he had an old tow sack from the barn, setting on the floor beside him. Stuffed full with things.

"You just ease on over and take one of them skillets and one of them sharp knives," Harrison said, pointing to the kitchen wares scattered in the soft glow of the hearth. "And watch yo' step. Go on, now, do what I'm tellin you, child."

Steal a skillet and a knife? Why would Harrison be taking things from the kitchen? Or cooking in the middle of the night? I started thinking that maybe he had gotten a little mixed up in his head. There were times he forgot that Old Master Hackler was long gone, or he didn't recollect right away what year it was, or he told me the same story over again. Could be this was one of those mixed-up times.

I didn't know what to do, though. If I hollered for Master or Miz Catherine, they'd come down, figure we were stealing around, and likely cowhide us both. But what would happen the next day when Lilly told Miz Catherine her skillet and knife had gone missing in the night? The redheaded devil would blame me sure enough because I was the one who slept in the kitchen. And then I'd have to tell how Harrison had gotten all mixed up and taken them, and he'd be in worse trouble.

I remembered Lilly telling about a cornfield slave named Willis John, who had worked in Master's fields years before. He had two fingers gone at the top knuckles because he'd stolen something when he was a boy. Tried on Old Master Hackler's hat, Lilly thought. She said getting the toppen part of your fingers cut off was some masters' punishment for blackfolks who took what didn't belong to them.

As I wrapped my fingers around the warm handle of the iron skillet and one of the best knives, the thought of what had happened to Willis John's fingers and what could happen to me, if Master or Miz Catherine saw me doing this, set my hands to trembling.

"Hurry, child," Harrison whispered, holding the door and waving his arms at me. "We gonna git caught if you don't hurry yo'self up." Not knowing what to do, I hugged the pieces close to my chest and followed him.

Outside, it was dark as a jar of ink. I couldn't even tell where the ground had gone to, and I nearly fell face-flat in the darkness, sending the skillet and knife clattering to the ground. Harrison clamped his hand around my arm. "Walk quiet, Samuel," he said low. But the ground felt strange under my bare feet, cold and prickly, with uneven places and crumbly, dry grass.

"Where we going to?" I tried to ask. "I don't want to get in no trouble with Master and Miz Catherine for bein out. I ain't s'posed to leave the kitchen at night. Lilly know what you doin?"

"Ain't got time for a hundred and one questions," Harrison

hissed, giving my arm a hard squeeze. "You just follow my say-so from now on. I got things all figured out."

I'd never been out of Master's house at night before. I wasn't allowed. Even if I had to use the old outhouse that belonged to Lilly, Harrison, and me, I wasn't to leave the kitchen at night, Miz Catherine said. Of course, it didn't much matter to me, because I didn't care for the darkness nohow.

Sometimes Lilly teased me about being scared of the dark, just to start a good argument when we were doing nothing but shelling peas or cutting up potatoes maybe. "You more afraid of the dark than the daylight is," she'd say.

"Maybe so," I'd tell her. "But human beings are supposed to be daylight people. Ain't that why they sleep at night?"

That would always make her laugh. "Then it sho' was a good thing you was born a human being. 'Cause if you was some ol' hoot owl or tree bat, you be in real trouble then."

But nothing good could come from wandering around in the night. I knew that. As Harrison crouched under each dark window of Master's house, I could feel those windows watching us. Same as Master Hackler's cold gray eyes. I held my breath as we passed the cracked-open back door with Cassius' boots standing on the top step. I half-expected the boots to come stomping down the steps after us. But they stayed where they were. Still and empty.

After that, Harrison hurried along the edge of the yard,

between the apple and peach trees that stood in dark rows. I'd never seen him move so fast, even when he got a scolding by Master Hackler for working too slow. Harrison always said that working in the fields, sunup to sundown for all those years, had worn out his leg bones until there was hardly nothing left to stand on. But his bones didn't look worn out to me anymore. He looked as strong as the field hands Master Hackler brought in every spring and fall.

Where was he in such a hurry to get to? I wondered.

And then, just beyond the row of bushes, I heard the low growl of a dog. Me and Harrison froze in our tracks. I knew trouble would find us, one way or another. Always does.

"You just stay where you is," Harrison whispered to me. "Don't make one sound." I watched as he slid his hand real slow into the tow sack and brought out something wrapped in cloth. Smoked meat, by the smell. He tossed a piece toward the bushes, and I heard the snap of teeth closing around it. There was a whole graveyard full of silence once the piece was gone. Was the dog waiting for us to move? Or was it holding its howling bark until we took one more step?

I could hear Harrison breathing fast.

Then a shadow hobbled toward us, swaying this-away and that-away as it came closer.

"Hallelujah." Harrison heaved a sigh, watching the dog come around the bushes. By the way it moved, I could tell right away who it was too. The only shadow that walked like that was Jake, Master's oldest hunting dog.

"Go on home, Jake." Harrison gave the yellow-skinned dog a soft slap on the ribs. "Go on home where you belongs. I don't have no more bones to toss away to you." Not paying us any mind, Jake took his good old time sniffing the whole tow sack, and smelling me and Harrison up and down, before he sidled away in the direction of the house.

Harrison reached into his bundle again. "S'pose this be as good a time as any to put these on our feet, Samuel." He held something toward me.

"Keeps the bloodhounds away," he said real low.

But I stared at the round onions in his hands as if they were hot coals straight from the Devil himself. This was the first time it dawned in my head why Harrison had brought a sack stuffed full of things. I had figured he was mixed up the way he sometimes was, or something had happened out in the fields.

But now I saw why he had warned me to keep my top eye open and why he had crept into the kitchen.

A grave walker's shiver went clear through me.

Harrison was planning to steal me from Master Hackler and Miz Catherine, and he was going to escape. Truth is, even the thought of going straight to hell didn't scare me as much as the thought of running away.

Onions

Harrison smacked my shoulder.

"Stop staring at me like you seen a ghost. Gimme the knife. You gotta put them on like this."

I watched Harrison's clumsy fingers slice off thick pieces of onion and reach for his feet, but his back was too stiff to bend far enough down. He cursed loudly and said, "You help me out here, child, and be quick about it."

I did what he told me. Scrubbed the strong-smelling onions all over his dark, knotted feet as if I was polishing the legs of Miz Catherine's parlor chairs, not fixing to run away. My fingers stung and my eyes burned so I couldn't even see what I was doing for all the tears.

"Ain't right to run off," I said under my breath. Lilly had always told me that running off was the surest way to bring the worst kind of trouble on my head.

Harrison straightened up and waved his hand toward the direction of the house. "Go on back to Mas'er and Miz Catherine then," he said sharply. "I ain't stoppin you." An owl hooted in the distance. I looked up at Harrison's face. His eyes were closed and he didn't have on any expression at all.

"Why you runnin away?" I asked.

"Die one way, die 'nother, soon enough."

"But they gonna send dogs after you. Young Mas Seth told

me about dogs that can hunt down runaways anywhere. Even two days after they gone. Even if they have run through water, he told me. What if they chase you down? You gonna get all tore up by them dogs."

"Why you think I brung the onions, Samuel? To keep them kinds of dogs away," Harrison snapped.

He stared at me and pressed his lips together. "I know what I'm doin. I lived long enough on this here earth to know what I'm doin when I decide to do something, you hear?" He was getting angry now. "You just make up yo' mind. Either you run away or you stay, but I'm goin, and the Devil's dogs can drag my old gray body back, arm by arm, leg by leg, if they want to." He glared at me. "You runnin off with me or not, Samuel?"

"Why you want to leave Lilly and me?" I pleaded.

" 'Cause I does," Harrison finished loudly.

"I'm afraid of you going, Harrison," I said, taking a swipe at the tears which were spilling out of my eyes, even though nobody was dying and Lilly would be ashamed of me again.

I could see nothing but terrible pictures in my mind. Mean bloodhounds being let loose on poor Harrison. Or Master laying open his back with lightning stripes. Pouring salt in each open stripe. That's what masters did to runaways. Terrible, unspeakable things, Lilly said.

"Tell you what. I got an idea." Harrison opened up the tow sack. "Why don't you put yo' fear in this here sack, Samuel? And say I carry it for you all the way north. And when us git there safe and sound, say I let it out, and it can float straight up into that free sky and be gone from us forever. How 'bout that?"

Harrison put on a wide, silly grin and waved his arms at the night sky. "Whooeeee, there goes all them things that be skeering the life outta poor Samuel all the time . . ."

"Ain't scared," I said.

"Know what that free sky is gonna look like, Samuel?" Harrison kept on. "Big, blue summer sky going from one end of the north to the other. 'Magine that. And blackfolks, they git to fly all around that sky. Don't that sound like something to see?"

I looked down at my feet.

Harrison picked up the tow sack.

"How far off is north?" I asked low.

"Ain't talkin no more," he said sharply. "You is just gonna start walkin with me and find out. I got my mind made up, Samuel."

And without another word, Harrison started off into the darkness, his long, skinny legs hobbling in a half-walk, half-run, past the horse barn, past the shadows of the henhouse, the corn-cribs, through the old apple orchard, around the field hands' cabin, and into Master Hackler's cornfields.

I followed him as if I had no more sense than one of Young Mas Seth's toys pulled on a string. In my mind, I could see Lilly shaking me as hard as she could when she found out, and saying, "How could you have gone and let ol' Harrison run off like that? And you went with him too? Here I figured you got more sense in yo' head than that. I raised you to know right from wrong. You shame me and your poor momma both."

But Harrison never stopped long enough for me to get a word in about Lilly or turning back. He hurried down row after row in the dark fields, until I lost count and couldn't have found my way back even if I had turned around.

Truth was, in my whole life, I had never gone this far away from anything. I had never been past Master's cornfields. The only thing that would have taken me beyond the cornfields, and over the low, rolling brown Kentucky hills, was a wagon carrying me to be sold off. So the thought of going outside Master's farm had always sent a shiver through me. Even Lilly, old as she was, had never left Master's farm, and three of her children hadn't either, because they were buried in our little Negro burying-ground past the field hands' cabins.

Only Harrison and the hired field hands had come from somewhere else. When he was young, Harrison had been bought from a Virginia farmer. "I recollect I was 'bout old enough to start workin in the fields when they sold me off. Maybe I was ten or eleven years," he had told me. But the only thing Harrison could remember of his old Virginia farm was a small pond where he once fished at night, thinking that everyone was asleep. Except, the master's son caught him. "Never done that again," he'd tell me for the hundredth time. "Never done that again."

- - -

As the sky lightened to gray, everything around us looked strange, like a dream that stirs up things you know with things you don't. The field we were standing in looked the same as Master's cornfield, but there was a board fence running along its edge, and Master used only split rail. And I saw a barn cat slip through the corn rows in front of us, but it was gray with two white feet, and our barn cats were all tabby-striped.

"Should be findin ourselves a hiding place," Harrison whispered. " 'Fore it gits too light."

I glanced up at the sky and thought about Lilly. She would be coming into the kitchen to get the fire started for cooking breakfast. "Samuel," she'd whisper, opening the door real slow, the way she did every morning. "Just ol' me here. You 'wake yet?" Lilly always said it was bad luck to scare a sleeping person out of their dreams, so that's why she kept quiet. But, truth was, I knew she didn't want us waking Master Hackler and Miz Catherine.

I squeezed my eyes shut, trying not to see her calling for me in the dark kitchen, not knowing I had gone.

"Samuel!" Harrison said louder, nodding in the direction of the woods. "You go on in there, and see if you can find us a big tree with a rotted hollow in the middle and three limbs low to the ground."

"Where?"

"Should be off that-aways," Harrison said, pointing. "Go on now, look, while I catch my breath."

I shot a glance at the dark woods. "I never been in them woods before."

Harrison glared at me. "Lord Almighty. You is never gonna earn your salt in this world, Samuel." Flinging the tow sack over his shoulder, he stalked past me. But we hadn't gone more than a stone's throw or two when I felt my skin raise up with gooseflesh.

There was an old maple with three limbs close to the ground. A raccoon hollow in the middle. And a lightning scar running down one side.

"Go on," Harrison said, pushing me forward. "There's the hiding place I was tellin you 'bout."

I stared at that old tree.

How had he known what the tree looked like before we got there?

Lilly said there were some folks who could foretell things in their minds. Things that were gonna happen. She believed in witching and spirits for bad things like cows going dry and hailstorms beating down the new corn. But the thought of Harrison using witching and spirits to help us run away put a chill in my blood. I wasn't about to go anywhere near that tree.

"What's got ahold of you?" said Harrison impatiently. "We gonna git some rest and hide ourselves here. Now, you come 'long, like I says. Stop being a child."

But I stayed where I was and watched Harrison shuffle toward the old tree. He took some cuts of onions and scattered them in the leaves.

"How'd you know 'bout this tree before we got here?" I ventured to ask, drawing a little closer. "You see things that happen 'fore they do?"

Harrison gave me a sharp look. "Don't know where you git all them foolish thoughts of yours, Samuel, but you better be leaving most of them in here," he said, tapping the top of my head with his finger, "where they belong, or they gonna git us in trouble, sho' enough. Know what I'm sayin?"

I stared at my feet stuck in the damp leaves, wishing more than anything that I was back fixing breakfast with Lilly. My mind laid it out on the table. A whole big plate of sizzling fatback and warm corn cakes.

Harrison traced his finger along the black lightning stripe. "If I could foretell things that were gonna happen in my life, you think I woulda worn out my bones workin for whitefolks all these years? No, I woulda rolled over and died the day I was born, that's what I woulda done."

Harrison looked over at me.

"Truth is," he said, calm as anything, "I run off once before, to this same tree. That's how I know it."

I stared wide-eyed at Harrison. Far as I knew, no one on Master Hackler's farm had ever stolen away. Especially not Harrison.

"You run away? From Mas Hackler?"

"A long, long time ago. From Old Mas Hackler. Way before you was born, Samuel." Harrison shot a hard look at me.

"And don't you go askin me no more about it, 'cause I ain't breathin another word. It's something between me and the good Lord, and that's all. Now, you help me git up to this here branch."

And without another word, Harrison started climbing into the tree himself. He made me pitch down on all fours so he could step on my back and pull himself up to the lowest branch. "I ain't nothin but an old sack of skin and bones," he kept telling me, but I thought he was going to split me in half like a fence rail while he was climbing up. After he was settled with a lot of cursing and groaning, I scrambled up to one of the other limbs.

We looked just like a pair of out-of-place birds perched in that tree. Harrison reminded me of one of those gray-headed birds, and I was one of those small, brown yard birds. Only we couldn't fly off, that's what I kept on thinking. If someone caught sight of us, we would have nowhere to go. We would be stuck in that old tree, nothing but a pair of helpless birds without wings.

"You think they gonna come after us?" I asked Harrison.

"Maybe so," Harrison answered, leaning his head back against the trunk.

"They gonna bring dogs?"

"Maybe so."

"That onion smell gonna cover where we walked?"

"Already tol' you that, Samuel. Onions and maybe a good hard rain."

I glanced up at the flecks of gray morning sky showing

between the leaves. It felt like rain, but no rain had fallen yet, and I remembered that my feet had sunk into the soft earth in more than a few places as we crossed the fields.

"You think this tree's gonna keep us hid from them dogs?" I asked, running my hand along the knotted bark.

"If they go round lookin for us, it will," Harrison answered.

"What if they find us? What's gonna happen?"

Harrison's eyes snapped open and he gave me his meanest stare. "Now, you be quiet, child, and git some rest 'cause we got another long run ahead of us. I don't want to hear no more of your talkin."

I kept quiet then, but the questions were still running back and forth in my head. What if I had left footprints in the field? What if Master hired dogs to track us down? What if it didn't rain? What if they found us sitting in the tree? What if they shot us down, as if we were nothing more than a pair of foolish wild birds?

I looked up at the sky and tried to make it rain. Rain. Rain. Rain. I wished as hard as I could. Lord, make it rain.

But then a sound interrupted my wishing.

"Samuel," a voice called sharply in the distance. "Samuel!"

Heart pounding, I closed my eyes and leaned back against the cold trunk of the tree. I knew whose voice it was . . .

They were already looking for us.

Still as a Tree

"OLD MAN, come out now!"

That was Cassius. He seemed to be riding along the line of the woods, looking in. I glanced over at Harrison, but his eyes were shut tight, and his mouth was moving in silent talking. Praying.

"SAMUEL! Where are you? Sam-uel!" The snake knotted itself around my throat as Master Hackler's voice slithered through the woods, looking for me. I squeezed tighter against the tree.

It was hard to tell for sure, but the voices seemed to be coming from the edge of the woods, near the field. Getting louder as they came closer.

Then came a voice I wasn't expecting.

"Samuel!" Lilly's familiar voice called for me. "Come on back now!" They had brought Lilly all the way from the kitchen to look for me.

I swallowed hard, thinking about the trouble I had surely brought to her. She had always barreled in to save me, and now I had gone and done the most shameful thing anyone could do. I had run off.

"SAMUEL! HARRISON!"

They were riding in our direction because I caught a glimpse of the brown flank of Master's horse and the bay-skinned mule with Lilly. I closed my eyes. I knew they were going to spot us, sure as anything, when they rode into the woods. And if I wanted to keep us from more trouble, I knew I had to call out for Lilly to save us. I didn't know how she'd keep me and Harrison from being cowhided for what we had done, but I knew there wasn't any other way out of trouble.

We all must pay, Lilly would tell me.

Maybe Miz Catherine would take the rest of Lilly's money and some of her saved-up things as punishment. Or maybe Master Hackler would listen to Lilly's talking because she had a way with him, she always said.

Drawing in a deep breath, I waved my arms and started to holler Lilly's name. "Lilly—" I called out.

But, at that moment, the loud crack of a rifle split the air.

"Lord, have mercy," I heard Harrison whisper.

In the silence after the gunshot, I pictured myself as still as a tree. I imagined that my arms and legs had turned into its branches, and that my brown skin was its dark, cold bark.

Three more shots rang out.

A warm drop trickled down my face.

I waited for the snapping of the underbrush as Master Hackler and Cassius made their way to our hiding place. I waited for them to catch hold of our ankles and pull us out of the tree.

Overhead the sky rumbled, and a sudden wind moved through the woods. Beneath me, the tree limb swayed.

My heart pounded. What was happening?

More drops fell on my arms. The sky rumbled again.

"Hallelujah!" I heard Harrison whisper. "Lord, let it rain!"

And then the rain came down. Hard.

It fell harder and harder, as if Master had shot holes in the sky. Big drops hissed on the leaves around us. And finally the rain fell in drenching white sheets, heavy as wet muslin on a clothesline.

Truth is, that rain saved us. When I squinted at the edge of the woods, Master Hackler, Lilly, and Cassius were gone. Harrison figured they hadn't seen us at all.

"Just trying to scare us," Harrison shouted above the noise of the rain. "But them shots 'bout took away the *last* years I got left!"

He didn't say a word about me hollering for Lilly. But I couldn't stop thinking about her sitting on Master's mule, calling out for me and Harrison. It made my insides hurt to picture it. Would Master take her back and cowhide her for letting us run off?

"What about Lilly?" I said. "She gonna be all right?"

"Lilly be fine," Harrison answered, pulling down his slouch-brimmed hat to keep the rain off. "She seen hard times before. She can take care of her ownself."

"Lilly know you was runnin off with me?"

"I reckon she knew I would run off sometime," Harrison said. "When the right time come. Don't you go worryin 'bout Lilly." He tugged a hat out of the tow sack. It was one of Seth's hats. "Forgot it in the barn, 'magine that!" Harrison grinned, holding the hat toward me.

I shook my head and kept on. "Why didn't she run off?"

"Who?"

"Lilly."

All Harrison would say was, "You got to be old like me and Lilly to understand things like that." Then he closed his eyes, leaned back against the tree trunk, and flat out refused to talk about it anymore.

All day, we sat up in that old tree while it poured. My legs kept falling asleep, and the rain ran in rivers down the tree limbs and soaked me clear through.

"I'm cold," I said about fifty times.

"Be thankful you ain't dead," Harrison answered from underneath his hat.

"When we climbin down?" I asked about fifty more times.

"When I says we does. Stop pestering."

I thought about Lilly working in Miz Catherine's warm, dry kitchen with the fire popping on the hearth. Lilly's big arms would be pressing out a tableful of dough, hands flying from the dough to the mound of flour and back, like brown birds dusting their wings. What would she be making? A couple of meat pies maybe. Or a Sunday pot of hens and dumplings.

My insides rumbled with hunger.

When I stood around too long watching Lilly work, she

would always press her lips together and give me one of her stares. "You spoiled to a stink," she'd tell me. "Git workin."

I looked nothing like Lilly. She had dark, high cheekbones and deep creases around her mouth and eyes. I was the color of ginger cake. "Just like your poor momma," she'd say. "I got the skin of an old, tough chestnut and you a nice piece of warm ginger cake." Thinking about Lilly made me sad, sad, sad inside.

"Don't let anything happen to her," I whispered to the sky. "She didn't do nothin wrong."

But the sky sent the rain splattering down even harder.

Night Scare

By the time the rain finally stopped, our muddy footprints had likely been washed clear to the Mississippi River. It was close to nightfall. The sun squeezed one last bit of light through the clouds, and Harrison pulled a handful of snap beans and four damp biscuits from his coat pocket. "Here," he said, giving me half. And that's all there was for our supper meal.

Truth is, I could have chewed up a whole field of snap beans and an entire plate of biscuits right then. I was that down-right hungry. And we had hardly brushed off the crumbs before Harrison decided it was time for us to be running again.

"**They** gonna be comin after us fast, now that the rain stopped," Harrison said, looking up at the evening sky. "But you gotta help me down from this tree, Samuel, 'cause I think rig-or mortis has set in both my legs."

I didn't know what "rig-or mortis" was, but my feet tingled and stung when they hit the ground, as if they had landed in a whole nest of bees. Then Harrison tried climbing down. Only, his knees gave way and his whole body sagged into the wet leaves. "If this ain't the most outrageoust thing," he swore, trying to stand back up again. "My mind wants to be free and my body don't."

Not knowing what to do, I stood there looking down at him.

"Stop staring at me, child," Harrison spat out. "Mind yo' business."

So I fixed my eyes on the silvery bark of the old maple. A black beetle was crawling along the rough tree, weaving back and forth. It had six needle-thin legs, and I pressed its shiny back, watching the legs churn by themselves.

I wondered how far we had to go 'til we got to freedom. What would happen if Harrison couldn't run any further?

"Now, Lord, if you can just raise up these bones of mine," I heard Harrison say. Out of the corner of my eye, I saw that he had found himself a crooked branch from the maple tree. With both hands curled around it, he was leaning and then standing. "I got my walking legs again," he said, breathing hard. He waved the walking stick at the forest. "Let's get a-movin, Samuel, before that rig-or mortis sets in again."

But as it got darker and darker, finding our way through the woods was worse than stumbling through a cluttered room without a candle. Roots reached up to tangle around our feet. Slippery mud and leaves sent me and Harrison pitching forward. Sharp twigs snapped across our arms and faces.

"I s'pose all the wild animals out there in them woods be laughing theyselves silly at the sight of us," Harrison sighed as he picked himself up and brushed himself off again. "You and me keep on falling flat in these woods as if we are both rum-drunk."

But as Harrison stood up, I had the feeling something was watching us. I remembered the big raccoons that used to tiptoe across Master's yard some evenings. And I knew snakes lived in the woods because Young Mas Seth had once brought home a big black one, stuck on the end of a stick. Even with its head cut off, this snake had been longer than Seth's arms stretched out. Seth said it ate rats. Which meant rats lived in the woods, too.

Then I felt something move in the darkness. Something that slid out from under my feet.

My heart dropped like a rock inside me, and I hollered for Harrison to run.

"Samuel!" he called out.

But I took off fast in the other direction. Branches snapped and rolled under my feet as I forgot all about being careful. Forgot all about being quiet. I could feel the wild animal right at my heels, chasing me. A snake. Or a big rat. Or something else. I ran as hard as I could, until I fell over a tree root in the darkness, and Harrison caught up.

"You hold on now," he hissed, snatching me up from the leaves. Above the noise of our hard breathing, I strained my ears to hear the sound of the animal sliding slowly out of the darkness toward us. I listened for the crackle of leaves and branches. But the only sound was the gentle creaking of the trees above us.

"Don't hear nothin," Harrison said, shaking my arm hard. "You just running like a scared rabbit, ain't you, Samuel? You never did see nothin in the woods, did you?"

"Yessir." My heart thudded in my chest. "Something big was followin us."

But Harrison just cursed at me and turned around in a slow circle. Looking up at the dark trees towering above us and the patch of night sky, he gave a low groan that sent a chill clear through me.

"Now you gone and done it, Samuel," he whispered. He sank down to the ground, covering his face with his hands. " 'Cause I done lost all recollection of the direction we was running in."

For the longest time, he just sat there on the cold, wet ground in the middle of the woods, saying nothing.

Feeling ashamed for running, I tried to tell him I would find the way back. "I bet I can find where we was. I got good sense. We ain't run that far."

But Harrison's eyes wouldn't even look up at me. They stayed closed. "Thirty-nine lashes," he whispered, his voice distant and trembly.

I leaned closer. "What?"

"Thirty-nine lashes for runnin off, law says."

"We ain't been caught."

"Old Mas Hackler says he gotta do what the law tells him to," Harrison mumbled. " 'You belong to me,' he says, 'just like my hunting dogs and my horses, and you get beat same as them if you run off. I don't like doin it, but I have to,' he says, ' 'cause you gotta learn to mind me.' "

"You mumbling, so I can't understand you, Harrison." I tried to pull on his shoulder. "Why you talkin about Old Mas Hackler?"

But Harrison turned away angrily. "Just let me lay here and

die," he snapped. "Don't put nothin on my back. I don't need none of your doctoring. Just let me lay here and die."

Harrison was talking out of his head. I thought maybe he had been stricken by a fever, or a delirium.

"Look up at the sky now," I said, pointing all around. "You think we can find our way yet?" But Harrison didn't even lift up his head.

"She didn't want to hide here," he whispered. "Belle tol' me the hayloft wasn't safe. And I didn't listen to her. And then the baby started up crying. Hushhh, baby." Harrison raised a finger to his lips. "Shhhh. . . ."

His words set me to trembling. Who was Harrison talking to? I didn't know anyone named Belle. And why was he worrying about hiding in a hayloft?

"Stop bein this way, Harrison," I pleaded.

I remembered how Lilly had gone out of her head like Harrison once. She took a hickory-splint basket she had made, one that she told me was her favorite, and threw it into the fire. She burned the whole basket to ashes without saying a word. Just told me to go away and leave her be. Even later, she wouldn't say what she was so awful sad about. "I got my thoughts, you got yours. Why you think the Lord gives us our own thoughts to keep?" is all she'd answer.

"You want me to leave you be?" I said to Harrison.

Around us, the woods were quiet, except for a splatter of raindrops as the wind came through the trees.

"Don't mind leaving," I whispered again.

Harrison was silent.

"You want me to go away?" I said louder.

He turned to me suddenly, giving me a look like his old self.

"Why you talking like that?" he snapped. "Where you planning on going to anyways?" He waved his hands at the woods around us. "They got wild animals out there. They gonna grab onto them skinny ankles of yours, pull you down, and chew yo' whole little body to pieces."

I didn't know if Harrison was trying to be funny or mean.

"Lordy, you as much trouble as your momma Hannah always was," he said, shaking his head. "Shoulda known."

Reaching into his pocket, Harrison pulled out a fat sweet potato. "May as well eat something. Nothin else to do," he said, cutting the potato in half. "Maybe you can use that fool head of yours to turn this into a slice of Lilly's good sweet-potato pie. If you can go 'round turning trees into wild animals, you oughta be able to do that." He handed me the sweet potato. "Lordy, Lordy, if only Lilly could see us now."

If she knew I had gotten us lost in the woods at night, running from a wild animal, she would be in a fit. I could hear her saying, "You always bringing us trouble we don't need, Samuel."

While I was finishing the sweet potato, Harrison opened his tow sack and drew out two blankets. I stared wide-eyed at those blankets because they looked like the same ones Master

Hackler had taken from me, saying, "Going cold ought to get to him too."

Harrison gave a slow grin and held up the striped wool blanket and the worn green one. "Ain't it a pity? Mas'er Hackler threw these two warm blankets out in the yard to get all wet and miry. Wonder who in the wide world they belongs to?"

The blankets smelled like Lilly's kitchen. Smelled of wood smoke and baking bread. Almost as if Lilly was setting right there with us. Harrison fixed the blankets around our shoulders, and we huddled beneath them like two snap peas inside a pod.

Beside me, Harrison gave a heavy sigh.

"You worrying 'bout us being lost?" I said, looking over.

"Naw."

"You think Mas Hackler is gonna find us tomorrow?"

Harrison stared into the dark woods. "Don't none of us know tomorrow," he said real quiet. "But we only run a mile or so, I figure. Or could be we circled right back to the tree where we started off. Too cloudy to see them stars now . . ." His voice trailed away.

"I'm sorry for what I done. I didn't mean to get us lost."

"Oh, hush now about that. Don't wanta hear no more." Harrison tugged at the blanket and turned away from me. "No use singing spirituals to a dead mule," he said sharply. "Now, git some rest."

Spiders and Candles

But I woke in the morning to find that Harrison had gone and left me. Same as if I was a dead mule.

My heart pounded. Had he run off while I was sleeping to save his ownself? White wisps of fog curled around the dark tree trunks. A sliver of early-morning sunlight cut through the trees. Overhead, crows called back and forth to each other. There was no sign of Harrison or the tow sack.

Did he leave me behind to be caught and taken back because I had been nothing but trouble? Or had he known that Master Hackler would rather find me because I was worth more than Harrison, who was old and worth almost nothing?

Lilly would have given me a crack across the face for even thinking that.

One time I had eavesdropped on Master Hackler bragging to a gentleman visitor about me. "Seven hundred dollars right there," he had said when I walked by. "Good, strong Negro boy grown up right."

All day I had walked around feeling as if my skin was made out of squares and squares of Lilly's Christmas dollars, all sewn together. But when I'd told Lilly what Master Hackler had said, she'd reached out and given me a hard slap across the mouth. "You oughta be ashamed of yo'self, Samuel. Lord, have mercy on your soul and your poor momma's too, for being proud of things like that."

That was the meanest thing I could remember Lilly ever doing to me. Later on, when we were boiling clothes in the wash pot and battling them on a stump to get the water out, she told me she was sorry for it. "But being worth money means being bought and sold. You understand that, Samuel?" she said, pointing her battling stick at me. "You proud of the fact that yo' black skin ain't no different than these clothes or this wash pot? You proud it's got a price, same as them?"

But sometimes I still thought about being worth a pile of money, more money than I had ever seen, because it made me feel important to be worth something big like that. Seven hundred dollars.

"You 'wake?" Harrison's voice startled me.

He came up quiet behind me and thumped my back with his walking stick. "Wondering if I run off without you, Samuel? Or you lookin out for more of them wild animals?"

"No, sir." I kept my eyes cast down, sure he could see what I'd been thinking.

"Time to be movin on." Harrison began gathering up my blankets and stuffing them inside the tow sack. "Quick now. 'Fore Mas'er Hackler and Cassius git themselves up and start nosing around."

I helped Harrison scatter leaves and brush so no one could tell where we had been sleeping. Unless, of course, the dogs found it.

"Can't do nothin about that," Harrison said, waving his arms. "If them dogs come, they gonna smell that we was sleepin there. They ain't fools." He tossed one last handful of leaves on the ground and moved the dirt around with his feet. "But you and me, I figure we jest lay low and hide ourselves for a time. Jest keep still all day, and maybe they won't come lookin for us." He pointed into the woods. "Found us a place to hide this mornin. Over there," he said, and started off through the trees.

But, it turned out, Harrison's hiding place was just a little thicket of weeds. Nothing more than what deer and rabbits hide themselves inside—and we weren't either one. Harrison poked his walking stick into the scratchy knot of goldenrod and jimsonweed and stirred up a cloud of white flies. "They gonna have to look high and low to find us here," he grinned. "Crawl in."

I went into the thicket slowly, waving my hand at the flies coming up from the ground in clouds. A spiderweb stuck across my face. I scrubbed my cheek, and it stuck to my hands. I rubbed my fingers on my trousers, my shirt, and the ground, trying to get that spiderweb off. Seemed as if unseen webs were sticking to everything on me, as if I was caught in a whole thicket of spiders and webs.

"Settle yo'self down now." Harrison gave me a poke with his walking stick. "Stop movin so much. Just stay where you is."

"I don't want to be in no weed patch full of spiders," I said under my breath.

"Be thankful it ain't full of dogs and whitefolks."

I pulled my knees up to my chest and stretched my shirt over my legs. Didn't want spiders crawling all over my skin. Nohow.

Sitting there, I thought about going back to Master Hackler's farm. I pictured how Miz Catherine would sweep into the kitchen in her silks. When she saw me, her eyes would fly wide open. "Samuel!" she'd say, looking surprised as Christmas. "You came back just like Lilly said you would."

Although, truth was, Miz Catherine was too fat to sweep into a room, and she almost never smiled. Most of the time, she kept her lips pressed so tight, they might have been stitched shut. And nearly everything she said to Lilly was mean. Breakfast was too late, too early, too hot, too cold, too overdone, too underdone, too sweet, or too filling.

Also, she liked to do mean things. One time, she let Young Mas Seth stick my finger in a burning candle because he wanted to see if it would turn white.

"Maybe underneath the black, their skin is white," Seth had said to his mother at breakfast one morning. "I want to know."

"Of course his skin isn't white," Miz Catherine snorted. "But stick his finger in the candle if you want to see for yourself."

So Seth had held my finger in the candle until the skin was all bubbled and burnt, and I was screaming and crying loud enough that Harrison heard me all the way in the barn.

"It ain't turning white," Seth said, finally letting go of my hand.

"Of course it isn't," Miz Catherine replied, calm as could be. "I told you they are black all the way through. Now, go tell Lilly to get him a cloth for his finger."

Strange thing was, I could always find the scar on my finger because it was almost white against my brown skin. So Miz Catherine had been wrong after all.

Twisting my finger this-away and that-away, I studied the small oval of gray-white skin. Thinking about it, I couldn't decide which was worse: running away with Harrison, and being hungry, lost, and covered in spiders—or staying with the red-headed devil Miz Catherine and Young Mas Seth for the rest of my life.

"You sleepin, Harrison?" I whispered over my shoulder.

"Naw."

"What you doing then?" I asked.

"Prayin," he answered. "I'm prayin all day that you and me be safe. You oughta be prayin too. Two prayers is better than one."

I stretched my shirt over my face and squeezed my eyes shut. Truth is, I said only one short prayer because Lilly always said the Lord didn't have time for people who carried on and on about themselves.

"Me and Harrison's been good, so far as I know," I whispered, breathing in my own hot breath. "We never hurt nobody, far as I know. Please keep us from being caught by dogs and being cowhided for what we done. We didn't mean to do nothin wrong."

But in the middle of my praying, there was the sound of something in the distance.

"Don't move atall," Harrison whispered.

Seemed like the sounds started coming from all directions after that, and you couldn't tell one from the other. A hundred far-off voices echoing inside a big kettle, that's what it sounded like. Were they after us?

An hour passed, maybe more.

The long-legged spiders crawled over me, and I didn't move. I stayed as still as the weeds. The voices swirled around us like water boiling, getting louder and softer, louder and softer. Everything scratched, and I wanted to holler and cry at the same time.

But, strange to say, nobody came into the thicket and found us. We lay in that weed bed from morning until night, and no dogs came to track us down. Maybe Master Hackler and the others were looking somewhere else. Or maybe the dogs couldn't find our trail with all the rain. Or maybe the praying worked. But even Harrison couldn't believe it.

"We been saved," he said as the last evening light melted into the weeds. "I don't know why, but this time, poor ol' me and you was saved."

I also noticed that the long-legged spiders had disappeared.

Two Fingers Gone

When it grew dark enough, we crawled out of the weeds and began to head north again, now that Harrison could see the stars in the night sky and had his senses back. All night, we hurried through woods and cornfields and along wide-open roads that made my heart thump in my chest when we crossed them. The moon was three-quarters full and stayed up most of the night, giving us a good bit of light to run by.

Come morning, we crawled into the middle of someone's cornfield to sleep and hide ourselves. Master Hackler's cornfields ran in straight, even rows. But this cornfield rolled back and forth, with rows going wide, then narrow, then real wide again. "Looks like somebody's plow horse was drinkin whiskey," Harrison chuckled as he peered down a row. "Never seen a field so crooked."

The ripe ears of corn still hung on the stalks too.

Harrison grinned and pulled off a few sweet young ears. "You and me's gonna eat forever and a day here. Yes, we is." Then he pulled a small stone jug of water and two apples from the tow sack. "Breakfast," he said.

"What else you got in there?" I asked, curious, because the sack still looked as full as when we started.

Harrison squinted at me. "Why you want to know so bad?"

" 'Cause I does."

"You been peeking inside of this sack when I wasn't lookin?" he asked, smacking the side of the tow sack with his palm.

"No, sir."

"All right, you git one look at what's inside, but you better keep yo' mouth shut about it." Harrison pointed his finger at me. "Anyone ever asks, you don't give them no bones, you hear?"

"Yessir," I answered.

"And stop saying 'sir, this' and 'sir, that,' or I'm a-gonna tie you inside this sack and carry you clear to freedom. You gonna git us caught, sho' enough. Lordy, Lordy."

Mumbling to himself, Harrison opened the tow sack and began to pull out what was inside. My eyes nearly went rolling out of my head when I saw what he had done.

The first things Harrison brought out of the tow sack were Master Hackler's riding boots with his big footprint still pressed into the fancy leather.

All the breath inside me was snuffed right out when I saw that. Those boots looked as black and mean as the night.

"I went and took Mas'er Hackler's riding boots for my ownself 'cause, well, it ain't something I can explain in words, I just did," Harrison said, setting the fancy black boots down in the field dirt.

He reached into the tow sack again. "And then I took Mas'er Hackler's best beaverskin hat. For you," he said, and held the hat toward me. "Here."

I felt the blood drain right down to my feet, but Harrison gave a little half-smile and smoothed the top of the hat with his hand. "Well," he said, pausing. "It's a mighty fine hat, anyways."

He set the hat next to me and reached back into the bundle. "And then I took an old bridle, in case us find ourselves a horse someday . . . and Cassius' silver pocket watch 'cause he was careless where he left it, and maybe we can sell it for money . . ."

By the time he was finished, he had pulled out an old green silk bonnet from Miz Catherine, a pair of riding gloves belonging to Cassius, Seth's worn hunting hat, my two blankets, Lilly's skillet and knife, a barn lantern and sulfur sticks, and a roll of gray wool yarn.

I felt the snake tighten around my throat as I stared at the pile of things Harrison had stolen from our master. If we were caught with them, we would be in worse trouble than I could even imagine. No one would believe me and Harrison owning a silver pocket watch or a pair of fancy boots. They'd know we were thieves and runaways for sure.

"You feeling poorly, Samuel?" Harrison asked curiously. "You givin me the strangest look."

"Why'd you go and take all them things?" I whispered, looking quick over my shoulder, as if Master Hackler was creeping through the field toward us right at that very moment. "They ain't ours."

Harrison snorted loudly. "Lord Almighty! Nothin BE-

LONGS to us, Samuel. Nothin in this whole world. Gotta have something good before I roll over and die, don't I?"

Tugging one of Cassius' white riding gloves over his hands, Harrison waved his fingers at me. "Lookee here, Samuel. I got all ten of my fingers, but see what's happened. Lordy, my hands done turned WHITE—pale as whitefolks' hands! What's poor ol' Harrison gonna do now?"

Even though I knew it was wrong, the sight of Harrison's old fingers half-stuck in Cassius' fancy white glove set me to grinning, then laughing. And while I was laughing, Harrison put Seth's hunting hat on my head and pulled it clear down over my eyes.

"Why, if it ain't Young Mas Seth!" he chuckled. "Dimwitted as his older brother. Can't even find his way outta a hat."

So I took Miz Catherine's bonnet, slipped it on Harrison's head, and tied the green bow under his gray-stubbled chin. "You the most outrageoust pretty lady I ever seen."

Harrison sucked in his cheeks and pouted his lips together. "You s'posed to call me MIZ Catherine," he mimicked.

Me and Harrison both fell facedown in the field dirt at that, and laughed until our sides ached. If Lilly could have seen us, she would have shaken her head and hollered at us for acting like two black fools, carrying on in the cornfield and making fun of Master and Miz Catherine. But we didn't care a straw.

- - -

We stayed in the field the whole day. When we weren't sleeping, we were lying back, cutting up, and doing nothing. Above the green corn, the skies were as clear and blue as I'd ever seen, and the air was full of the warm smell of cornstalks baking in the sun. I lay back on the dirt and breathed it all in, feeling as if the world had forgotten about me and Harrison.

It did feel awful strange to be gone so long from Master Hackler and Miz Catherine, though. Especially when I knew I was supposed to be carrying the slop jars to the outhouses, raking up the barn lot, collecting the eggs, feeding the hogs, filling the water buckets, and plucking the chickens Lilly would need for supper. By my count, we had been away almost three whole days. Who was taking care of all my work?

I even started to wonder whether me and Harrison had somehow passed on to the Promised Land, the way folks do when they die. Maybe that's why nobody had found us.

"You think we died and gone into the Promised Land?" I asked Harrison while we chewed on some ears of corn. It was near evening, and we were waiting for the dark to run again. "That why no one's come lookin for us?"

Harrison gave a low chuckle and looked over at me. "When I pass on to the Promised Land, Samuel, you think I'm gonna bring this old, crippley body with me?"

I squinted at his wrinkled-up skin, and the bushy crown of gray hair circling his head. "No, I s'pose not." I grinned.

"But I got a feeling that tonight you and me is gonna git

ourselves somewhere closer to the Promised Land." With his ear
of corn, Harrison solemnly pointed into the distance. "See, when
you find the River Jordan at the top edge of Kentucky, you is
halfways to Canaday, they say."

"Who says?"

"Folks I heard talking, one time or another. I got two ears,
you know," Harrison said, rolling his eyes. "And we gonna find
that river tonight, I got a feeling."

I remembered Lilly telling me about the River Jordan.
Almost every river in the Bible was named Jordan, seemed like.
Jordan or the Red Sea. On Sundays, Lilly would always read out
loud from her little Bible. "Same as I did for my own flesh and
blood," she'd say. Only, truth was, Lilly couldn't read a word,
same as all of us. She would just turn to a page and tell the stories
she had saved up in her head. "But I knows what's written down
there," she would always say, tapping her finger on the page.
"Don't need to see it to read."

"The River Jordan's a real river?" I asked.

Harrison cut his eyes at me. "You sayin the river I'm talking
'bout ain't real?"

I just put my head down then and chewed on my ear of
corn. Let old Harrison think what he wanted.

With his finger, Harrison drew a crooked line in the cornfield dirt. "Say this is the Ohio River right here," Harrison said,
tapping the dirt with his finger. "Blackfolks, see, they call it the
River Jordan, and whitefolks, see, they call it the Ohio River."

Harrison looked up. "If you ask me, blackfolks should name everything in this world. Don't know why whitefolks use the kinda names they do. Look at poor ol' Noah," Harrison continued. "He goes and spends all them forty days and forty nights on water, and have you heard of whitefolks naming one little river after him?"

I shook my head.

"There now, that don't make no sense, if you ask me . . ."

As Harrison kept talking, I thought about the River Jordan winding through our green cornfield, carrying Noah and his family in a big ark. Only, in my picture it was me and Harrison and Lilly in that big ark . . .

River of Death

That night, just after the sun set, me and Harrison started looking for the River Jordan. We pushed our way through the crooked rows of corn, and when we got to the edge of the field, we sat down in the weeds, waiting for more darkness to come. Above our heads, the sky was the color of huckleberries—blue, almost black.

"What's the River Jordan gonna look like?" I asked Harrison. He was sitting in the field dirt next to me, with his arms resting across his knees. Eyes closed.

"Don't know," he said slowly. "See it when I git there, I reckon."

"How you gonna know it if you never seen it before?"

Harrison waved his arm at the field around us. "You and me, we just look for a big, wide river with a mess of lights on the other side. That's how we know."

"Say there's lots of rivers like that," I said, picking at the corn kernels stuck in my back teeth. "How you gonna know for sure which one is which one?"

Harrison stood up and swung the tow sack over his shoulder, not saying a word.

"Say we find the Miss'ippi instead?" I kept on. "If we ain't seen it before, how we gonna know for sure?"

"STOP PICKIN YOUR TEETH," Harrison hissed, pointing his finger at me. "And stop being smart with me. I don't wanta hear no more of yo' talkin, Samuel. I does the bossing and you does the following 'round here." He stomped past me, crushing stalks of corn and weeds under his feet. "You just hush up," he said, turning to look back at me. "HUSH UP and don't talk to me no more about the Miss'ippi River, you hear?"

I didn't dare to breathe another word. I just followed Harrison as quiet as I could, trying not to get his dander up. We walked out of the cornfield and into a small woods. And truth is, we found a river almost right away, so Harrison must have known what he was looking for after all.

There was a line of trees just past the cornfield where we had hidden ourselves, and beyond the trees the land started to roll downward. As me and Harrison slowly picked our way down the steep hillside, I could hear the soft sound of water flowing somewhere in the darkness.

But the hill we were walking down ended at nothing more than a creek. There were no lights showing at all on the other side. It was just brush and thick trees. Rocks and fallen branches poked up, here and there, in the shallow water. Was this the River Jordan we were looking for?

"You just ease yo'self down to the water first, Samuel." Harrison pointed at the edge of the riverbank. "Then you help me down there so I can git a good look."

But as my feet slid down the small riverbank, I got a lungful of something awful bad coming up from that water. Smelled like rotten fish or dead animal to me. Standing beside the river, I pressed my arm across my whole face, breathing through my shirt cloth. Harrison's feet landed with a soft sound next to me.

"You smell that?" I said, shifting from one foot to the other. "We ain't gonna stay here, right?"

Harrison didn't answer, just steadied himself on my shoulder.

"Don't that water smell awful bad? Don't it smell like something's dead round here? You think something's dead, huh?" I whispered loudly, trying to see up and down the river.

"Hush." Harrison gave me a smack on the arm. "I can't even hear my ownself think."

I shut my mouth then and tried not to think about what might be dead in the river: A shot deer? An old horse? A dead person? A whole mess of dead people? My throat felt tight all of a sudden like I was going to be sick.

"Let's move somewhere else, Harrison," I said, tugging on his arm. "Don't like it here atall."

"I'm thinking 'bout what to do. Stop pestering me." Harrison reached down to pick up one of the river stones. "You figure this is the wrong river?" he said, turning the river stone over and over in his palm as if it might tell him where we were supposed to be.

"Can't we just find another river?" I asked.

I didn't care if it was the wrong river or the right river. Only thing I knew for sure is that I didn't want to set one foot in that dark water. Even if it was the River Jordan. Even if Moses himself was waiting on the other side.

"Why?"

" 'Cause it don't look like the River Jordan to me. You said there'd be lights on the other side. I don't see no lights."

"All right," Harrison said, as if he had made up his mind. "Then I guess we just cross over this little river and keep going north. Maybe we got the wrong river. Maybe another one will come along. Maybe it'll look like they said."

I stared down at the black water and folded my arms, stubborn as a stump. "I ain't goin in that water. Nohow. Not with the way it smells. Not with something dead floating in it."

"Don't be a child," Harrison said sharply. "Lemme grab ahold of your shoulder." Digging his old fingers into my skin, he said, "You gonna help me git across. That's all there is to it. We gonna cross this river and keep going north." He began to push me into the dark pools of flowing water as if I was nothing more than his old walking stick. "Go on, now," he said. "Go on. Start walkin. WALK—"

With Harrison behind me, I couldn't do a thing. My feet slid on the slabs of rock as he pushed me right into the river. "Stop goin so slow," he hissed, squeezing my shoulder. Staring into water as black as midnight, I tried to slide my feet across the bottom, one foot at a time, because I wasn't about to step on anything dead. But each time I stepped down, the slick, muddy rocks made my heart fall right to my feet.

In the middle of the river, the water swirled past my knees, taking my breath away.

"Lordy. Lordy. Lordy . . . ," Harrison whispered, and I felt his fingers tighten on my shoulder. "Keep movin, Samuel," he said, pushing me.

Seemed like it took half the night to pick my way across, with the darkness and the rocks and Harrison. I never did see what was dead, although the smell was worst where the water was deepest, so the dark river must have been hiding something terrible beneath it.

When we finally reached the other side, I left Harrison to pull his old self up the steep riverbank. Figured if he could push me across the river, he could do that by himself. I sat down on a log at the top of the riverbank and waited for him.

But when Harrison finally got to where I was sitting, all he said was, "We don't die but once," in a hard voice, and then he kept right on walking. Past me. Not even looking back.

Made me just want to stay there and let him leave. Let him stumble around in the dark by his ownself.

We don't die but once. What was that supposed to mean?

And where was he going off to? There was no River Jordan—that's what my mind said. We were just wandering and wandering in a dark, tangled woods, looking for a river we would never find. And, truth is, how could you find something you had never seen?

I remembered when Miz Catherine had lost a pin that belonged to her dead mother. She made us crawl across all of the floors in the house looking for it—even Lilly she ordered onto her hands and knees. And while we crawled, Miz Catherine stood over us and poked us hard with the toe of her shoe.

"I know you go through my fancy things when I'm out," she said, her mean voice rising higher and higher. "You know what my mother's pin looks like. Don't tell me you haven't seen it." But we didn't have the smallest idea what we were looking for. Gold, silver, pearl? We never found any pin at all, so Miz Catherine took something from each of us—Lilly's good Sunday bonnet, a pair of winter gloves from Harrison, and a set of clay marbles from me—saying if we stole from her, she would steal from us. "But you can't find things you never seen." That's what Lilly kept trying to tell her.

And I wanted to say the same thing to Harrison, but he wouldn't listen to any sense. Wouldn't stop looking for that old River Jordan. He shuffled up the hillside away from the river, not speaking a word to me. Just kept driving his walking stick hard into the ground, as if he was trying to plant beans in a field.

We crossed over a narrow mud path, through a small field of tobacco, past a barn that looked tumbledown and empty, around a stone wall, and into another thick woods. Still going uphill.

Seemed like the uphill went on forever.

And then it stopped.

"The River Jordan," Harrison whispered. "There it is, Samuel. Just like they says."

Below us, the land fell away to a blanket of deeper shadows with pinpricks of light scattered here and there. Looked like nothing but a handful of little fireflies thrown into the darkness.

Setting down the tow sack, Harrison raised his hands in the air like he was praying to the night sky. "Hallelujah," he said in a trembling way that sounded both scared and pleased at the same time. "Ol' Harrison finally made it to the River Jordan."

"I don't see no river," I said, squinting into the darkness.

"Listen," Harrison whispered.

I slapped at a mosquito and listened to the still, quiet air. A dog barked somewhere in the distance, and a night bird called out nearby, but I couldn't hear water flowing. Not even a drop of water. "Don't hear a thing," I tried to say.

"A big river ain't like Lilly's kitchen pump," Harrison hissed. "You ain't gonna hear water pouring out of the ground. Use yo' ears and listen now." It was the same soft sound as the wind brushing across a field, he said, or thunder from far-off clouds rumbling through the sky. "Listen for a small sound moving across something big. Hush, now. Just listen," he told me.

But I still didn't hear any river.

Harrison pointed toward the deeper darkness just below us. "See how the land goes down, Samuel? Goes down to the bottomlands around the River Jordan. And them bottomlands is flat as my hand, flat as the top of a table. They call them the Cornfield Bottoms, 'cause they's full of corn growing from the blackest, flattest earth you ever come across."

Harrison was quiet for a long while, just staring toward that river we couldn't see. I thought maybe he had forgotten where he was.

"We gonna keep movin?" I said real low.

Harrison shook his head. "You don't know nothing 'bout what's waiting for us in them bottomlands, Samuel." He pointed his walking stick at the darkness. "Them cornfields is full of patrols. Whitefolks down there, they hunt flesh-and-blood people. Got guns and dogs and whatever else they can find to catch blackfolks. Hunting you and me ain't no different than trapping animals to them."

A chill went through me. I remembered something Young Mas Seth had told me once. I was collecting some eggs from the henhouse, and he had peeked around the door. "My brother knows a fellow who hunts runaway Negroes on the border of Kentucky," he'd said. "They call him a pat-er-roller. He caught twenty-two Negroes in one week. You ever heard of pat-er-rollers before?"

"No, sir. Now, you go away from me," I had warned him.

But he waved his wooden popgun at me like he was something big. "They pay a hundred dollars a runaway there. If I hunted Negroes, I bet I'd be as rich as a king. Maybe if you run off someday," he said, pointing the gun, "I'll hunt for you."

"Ain't running away," I told him. "Now, stop telling me stories."

But he popped a hard cherry pit at my back anyway. "Bang. You're dead." He laughed and ran off.

Later, when I asked Lilly about patrollers, she turned around real fast and pointed her finger at me. "You just stay away from Seth and do the work you got to do. Stop listenin to all his foolish stories. There's lies growing outta every hair on his head."

But maybe what Seth had said was true.

Digging through the tow sack, Harrison pulled out Lilly's sharp knife. The one I had taken from the kitchen. "That's why I brung this along," he said.

My voice stuck in my throat. "Why?"

Harrison waved the knife at me. " 'Cause if somethin happens, if they catch us down there, I ain't going back to Mas'er Hackler. I'll slit my own throat ear to ear 'fore they take me back." Harrison's eyes had that look in them again, the same wild-eyed look from the woods.

"I been caught once, and they ain't never catchin me again," he whispered. "Ol' Harrison, he'll fight 'til he's dead and gone."

Cornfield Bottoms

They hunt people who run off from their masters. Human flesh and blood. Hunting you and me ain't no different than trapping animals to them. I'll fight 'til I'm dead and gone . . .

Harrison's words tumbled through my mind as we crept down the dark hillside toward the Cornfield Bottoms and the scattering of lights that Harrison called the River Jordan. We walked carefully, the way deer slip through the woods, placing each foot softly in front of the other, freezing at the smallest sound—the snap of a twig, a clatter of stones, a dry whisper of leaves.

In the middle of the hillside, I stopped and stared at a shadow in front of us, thinking it was a patroller. He was crouched behind a clump of low bushes with a rifle sitting across his knees and a dog curled at his feet. My heart pounded.

"You see something?" Harrison held tight on my arm, breathing fast.

"Over there," I said, nodding.

As the moon came out of the clouds, Harrison shook his head and whispered, "Ain't nothin there. Just a tree."

But in the darkness, everything looked strange and mean, as if the whole hillside was trying to catch us. I was jumpy as spit on a hot skillet as we crept down through a real thin patch of small trees. The moonlight slipped in and out of pale clouds, playing tricks. Branches stuck out like rifles. Low bushes looked like bloodhounds, ready to spring.

"Don't like this atall." Harrison's voice shook. "Not atall."

And then we nearly stepped onto the ashes of a still-smoking fire.

"Git down," Harrison hissed, and we dove to the ground.

A broken clay pipe and a few chicken bones, not even burned yet, lay scattered in the glowing embers in front of us. A pile of kindling and leaves waited nearby, ready to be stuck in the fire. A man's glove rested on one of the warm stones—

Me and Harrison didn't stay to see another thing.

On our hands and knees, we crawled slowly toward a dark cornfield ahead, not saying a word until the cornstalks swallowed us up. Breathing hard and listening to the sound of our own thumping hearts, me and Harrison lay facedown among the tangled legs of corn.

Who had built the fire? Were they patrollers? Hunters? Were they lying in wait for runaways? Or hiding somewhere in the cornfield?

Motioning for me to follow him, Harrison stood up and began to creep farther away from the fire. Softly, he pushed the scratchy cornstalks aside with his hands, going down row after row, as if he was moving through deep water.

Above the scratching of the corn rows, I heard far-off

noises—a gunshot echoing, a woman's voice hollering, a dog barking, a cowbell—but near us everything stayed still and empty, not a living soul around, it seemed like.

The land had become flat as a tabletop, just as Harrison had said, and as we walked and crawled in the darkness, my feet pressed into clods of soft, damp-smelling earth. Mosquitoes buzzed in my ears. But I was listening so hard for the sound of whitefolks or dogs that I didn't notice the river until we were almost on top of it. Even then, I didn't hear the sound of it; the cornstalks just fell away to a rippling field of black and silver in front of us.

"Lord Almighty," Harrison said softly, sinking down to his knees on the grassy riverbank. "We have found the River Jordan."

The river in front of me and Harrison was nothing like the one in Lilly's stories. I stared at the water, not believing my eyes. The river was as deep and black as the night sky, and the pinprick row of lights on the other side looked as far-off as the old moon.

Right then, I knew we had come to the end of our running away from Master Hackler because it was plain to see that no matter how far we walked along the wide River Jordan we would never find a place to cross it.

But Harrison didn't seem to realize that there was nowhere to go. Digging through the tow sack, he pulled out the tin barn lantern.

"Where you going to?" I asked.

"Where you think?" he said, calm as anything. "Into that river."

My heart pounded as I watched him light his lantern with a sulfur stick and make his way slowly down the riverbank. Then, without turning around or saying a word, he lifted up the lantern and walked straight into the water!

I am ashamed to say I squeezed my eyes shut after that. I believed, sure as anything, he was going to keep on walking until he sank slowly below the dark water—first his legs, next his chest, then his shoulders and his head, and finally the glow of the lantern—swallowed up by the River Jordan.

"Samuel," Harrison hissed loudly. "SAMUEL!" I opened one eye. Harrison stood waist-deep in the black water. "Don't just stand there like you is turned to stone. What's got ahold of you? Git yo'self out here in this river with me."

"We can't go across the river like that, Harrison," I tried to tell him.

"Who says?" Harrison flapped his arms like wings above the water and the lantern bobbed crazily, up and down, in the darkness. "You and me is gonna turn into owls and fly away." Holding the lantern high in one hand, and cupping his other hand around his mouth, Harrison gave a loud hoot that echoed across the water. "Who-who-who-whooo . . ."

All the skin on my arms rose up with gooseflesh because I knew that Harrison had gone out of his head. He had fallen into a fit at the sight of the wide river we couldn't cross, and in his delirium, he was going to get us caught.

"WHO-WHO-WHO-whoooo." Harrison turned and hollered again, loud as a drunken man.

"Harrison," I tried calling out soft. "Come on back now." I held my breath, waiting for whitefolks to spring out of the cornfields and barrel down the riverbank toward us.

"Who-who-who-whooooo . . ." Harrison kept on, not paying me any mind. "You hear them owls answering me back, Samuel?" He waded into the shallower water near the riverbank. "I keep on listenin and I ain't heard a thing yet, how 'bout you?"

"There's nothin out there. You is just 'magining things," I said, shaking my head and feeling downright sick inside because I knew there were no owls coming to carry us across the river. Only in Harrison's mixed-up mind. "Stop hollering like that, and come on out of the water now," I begged.

"Hush. I believe I just heard an owl, child." Harrison put his finger to his lips and looked up at the night sky. He turned his head this-away and then that-away, as if he was expecting owls to come flying over at any moment.

Sinking down among the tangle of weeds along the riverbank, I hugged my knees to my chest. What would Lilly tell me to do with trouble like this? What would she say to do about Harrison being out of his head, the cornfields being full of patrollers, and the river being too wide to cross?

The river water slapped gently on the shore as the wind came up.

It made me think of Lilly slapping the water out of the clothes when she washed them. Her hair would be tied up in a yellow headwrap, and her rolled-up sleeves would look like thick rings of dough around each arm. She would heave a sigh and say, "You got yo'self in a mess a' trouble this time, Samuel. And a whole washtub of water ain't gonna make it come clean, that's for sho' . . ."

But then I heard another sound.

Close by, an owl called soft and low.

Only this time it wasn't Harrison.

The River Man

"Hallelujah!" Harrison whispered, swinging the lantern back and forth, high above the dark water. "The river owl has come for us. Git the tow sack and git a-movin, Samuel." He splashed out of the water toward me.

I squinted into the darkness, trying to see what strange kind of bird was coming to save us. Even though I knew it was downright foolish, I conjured up a picture of a big, silver owl flapping across the River Jordan and plucking us from the riverbank just as a crowd of white patrollers burst out of the cornfields with their dogs and their guns.

But what came out of the darkness was not an owl at all, of course. As we stood on the riverbank, an old rowboat slid out of the shadows. In the moonlight, I could see the silver ripple of its oars in the water and the dark shape of someone sitting in the middle. The way that shape looked, whoever was sitting in that boat was big. Powerful big.

"Go on, help him come in, Samuel," Harrison whispered. Raising the lantern for light, he pointed toward the water's edge. "There, where I was standin."

The rowboat drew nearer to us, and I could see that it was a colored man's arms pulling hard on the oars. But as the boat slid into the mud bank, I noticed something strange about those arms. White marks and lines cut all over them, and patches of white skin like my scar covered the large hands wrapped around the oars.

Without turning around, the river man swung the oars into the boat and stood up slowly. Seemed as if he didn't just stand up, he rose up. Like haunts do. His shadow unfolded from that little rowboat, getting bigger and bigger.

I drew in my breath.

One leg stepped down into the river, making a ripple in the water, and then the other. The man held the side of the rowboat and turned to face us.

And my heart stopped dead inside me.

Lines cut across the colored man's whole face. It looked as if someone had stitched together the pieces of his skin. White scars ran from his mouth to his right eye, from his lower lip to his chin, from his eyebrow across his wide, brown forehead. And as I stared at him, the pieces seemed to shift and move. In the flickering glow of Harrison's lantern, white teeth became eyes, a cheek sagged into the skin, one nose became two, broken lips moved together, a scar made a strange half-smile.

Then the man spoke. Sounded like deep thunder rumbling.

"Not a night for some black boy to be wandering along the Ohio River." The man fixed his eyes on me. " 'Specially without any way to get himself across."

My tongue felt as if it had turned to ashes.

The river man's dark eyes shifted to Harrison, who hadn't

moved from where he stood, still holding the lantern up in the air. "You trying to get across this river, too, old man?"

"Don't know," Harrison answered, his voice hardly above a whisper. Staring at the man's face, he took an unsteady step backward, breathing loud.

"You don't know?" the man repeated. "Skin as black as earth, body bent over from doing whitefolks' work all your life, and you don't know what you're running from, old man?"

With a deep, rolling chuckle to himself, the river man reached for something on the bottom of the rowboat, something hidden in the shadows. Even before he quickly raised it and pointed, I saw what it was. My heart roared in my ears.

A pistol.

"You listen to me now, or I'll leave you just where you are and save myself, you hear?" the man's voice rumbled. "I don't have time for confused old men or chickenhearted boys. You want to go across this river with me or not, old man?" He leveled the gun at Harrison.

Voice trembling, Harrison said he did.

"And you?" The man stared at me from his scar-ruined face.

I nodded my head, not daring to open my mouth, not even daring to breathe.

"All right, then." The river man waved his pistol at me and Harrison. "This is for folks who don't do what I tell them, don't move fast enough, or don't keep hushed enough. Understand? I got a price on my head, ten times the price on yours. And your death doesn't mean near as much to me as mine. Understand?

"So, get in." The man pointed the pistol at Harrison. "You first."

Like a wooden toy, Harrison moved stiffly through the water and climbed into the front of the boat. He sat down on the seat and folded his hands like he was praying. "Git the tow sack and climb in, Samuel," Harrison said, looking down. "Ain't nothin to be skeered of." But I could tell he didn't believe a word.

And when I climbed into the boat, I saw why. There, on the man's seat, lay an unsheathed knife as long as my arm, and on the floor of the little rowboat rested a black-handled club. And if this wasn't trouble enough, we had hardly left the riverbank when a woman's scream split the air.

Hetty Scott

The scream came from the direction of the cornfields, and after it, I could hear the muffled echo of gunshots and the sad, bawling sound of hunting dogs chasing something through the fields. Cursing, the river man leaned back and pulled hard on the oars. Only thing me and Harrison could see was the dark wall of his shoulders in front of us, coming back and going forward, pulling hard as he could on those oars. Trying to get us into the river. Fast.

Hugging my arms around my knees, I hunched down as the old boat creaked and rocked into the shallows. The water thumped on the wooden sides, and sounded just like a hundred terrible hands knocking to come in.

Another scream came across the field, closer this time.

"Put out your lantern," the man hissed over his shoulder. Water splattered over us as he swung the oars out of the water. Harrison fumbled with the catch of the lantern, trying to open it.

"I told you to put out that lantern," the man snapped. Turning around suddenly, he smacked the lantern out of Harrison's hands. It clattered onto the wet floorboards of the boat, sputtering and hissing. Harrison gasped sharp, and then grew quiet. Keeping his head down, he whispered, "Don't you worry, Samuel. Everything's gonna be all right."

But nothing was going to be all right. I knew that.

I could hear the sounds of a terrible chase coming from the cornfield—the crack of gunshots, hunting dogs bawling and chopping, men hollering, "Here, over here . . ." Sounded as if they were chasing someone toward the riverbank, same as they tree a raccoon or corner a fox.

Then a clear voice came from the edge of the river. "Somebody out there, help me." It was a colored woman's voice, sure as anything. "Help me!" she called.

"Don't you say a word," the man whispered over his shoulder to us. "We are just gonna sit here quiet and leave that woman be."

Our boat drifted like a leaf on the water, and I looked up at the silent, hunched-over shadow of the man in front of us. A shiver of fear went straight through me. He was bigger than me and Harrison put together. What would happen to us? "Your death doesn't mean near as much to me as mine," wasn't that what he had said?

The woman on the riverbank called out again. Her voice was terrible and sad enough to harrow up the soul. I could hear the men in the cornfield getting louder. They would catch her in no time.

"Help me, somebody out there, help me, help meeeeeee . . ."

The river man swore under his breath. Then I heard the oars hit the water as he swung them into the river. Leaning his shoulders into the oars, the man turned the boat. But instead of moving deeper into the river shadows, he pulled straight for the shore.

We smacked hard into the same riverbank we had left from, and the man climbed out so fast it seemed as if he was trying to throw us all into the water.

"Over here, woman, over here," he called, spitting out a string of curses into the darkness.

Next thing I saw was a cloud of fancy clothing in his arms. It tumbled into the other end of the boat—layers and layers of clothing, with two brown hands and a pair of fancy ladies' slippers waving and kicking. The cloud stank to high heaven of flower perfume.

"Careful of them pretty dresses," a voice babbled from deep in the clothes. But the river man splashed into the boat, splattering mud and water everywhere. He sat down in the middle and put his muddy boots right in the heap of fancy clothing. As far as I could see, there wasn't room anywhere else. Not with me and Harrison on one end, and the lady piled on the other.

"Lordy, I'm a-shakin like a leaf," the lady's voice kept on talking. "My name's Hetty Scott," she said, fluttering her brown hands in the air. "I run off from my mistress and they's all chasing me. I don't know how much further I coulda run in Miz Emma's fan—"

But the rest of Hetty Scott's words were frozen in the air as four dark shadows came tumbling down the riverbank into the water.

Bloodhounds.

And right behind the dogs, there was the sudden glow of lanterns and torches coming out of the field like eyes. Men hollered and ran toward the riverbank, pointing at us.

"Lord, save us," Hetty Scott wailed.

The river man's voice thundered, "Get down, get down," as he leaned into the oars. There was the crack of gunshots from the shore, and a sound like stones being skipped across the water. Only, I knew it wasn't stones.

"Put yo' head down, Samuel," Harrison hollered, pushing my head so hard that my chin smacked into my knees. More stones skipped across the water, and I whispered for Lilly to save us.

Seemed like we were slowly slipping beneath the river. Cold water seeped through the knee cloth of my trousers, and I could hear water knocking on the sides of the rowboat. There were muffled sounds above. Harrison and the river man hollering. A dog yelping. Sounded like they had brought an oar down on one of the bloodhounds. There were more rifle shots, farther off, and then everything faded and grew quiet around us.

"You still down there, Samuel?" I could feel Harrison lean over me.

"Samuel." He gave my arm a hard shake.

I opened my eyes one at a time, making sure the night sky was still up there and the sides of the old rowboat were still around us. Had we got away?

"They gone?" I said, looking around. The river man had his oars out of the water, listening too. I could hear the sound of the lady in the back of the boat, crying loud, and I thought about Lilly telling me, "You ain't allowed to cry unless folks is dying or dead." The way that lady was crying on and on would make you think that we were all dying or dead.

"She hurt?" I asked.

"Naw . . ." Harrison grinned and shook his head back and forth. "Ain't nothin wrong with her—" He lowered his voice to a whisper. "But she sho' do smell, don't she?" He waved his hand at the back of the boat. "Whoooeeee. Wonder where she stole all that fancy perfumery?"

A loud ripple of laughter came flying out of my mouth.

"You think getting away with your life is something to be laughing about, boy?" The river man turned quick. "Well, you just keep on laughing." Then, with a smack of his oar, he hit me and Harrison with a wave of river water, hard as a hand slap.

As me and Harrison gasped for air, the river man's voice rumbled low and mean. "Your two scraps of life ain't worth a thing. Not one thing to whitefolks." He squeezed my arm and pointed into the darkness. "You are gonna get to the other side of this river, boy, and open up your hand, and what are you gonna see inside of it? Nothing. See if you laugh then," he said. "See if you laugh then."

My eyes stung with tears as the man turned back to his

oars. He was as mean as a snake. Even meaner maybe. I couldn't figure out why he had gone and saved us from the patrollers and why he was rowing us across the river. He didn't care a straw about us. Not one straw.

Harrison kept his head down, not saying another word. But I could hear Hetty Scott still softly babbling and crying to herself.

The man leaned over her heap of clothes. "Don't want to hear another sound from you, or I'm gonna toss you and your clothes in the river, you hear me?" he said harshly, and Hetty Scott's crying dried up quick as water.

Breathing hard, the man kept on rowing up the river. Far-off voices drifted across the rippling blanket of water. In the night air, I could smell wood smoke and a sharp iron smell that made me think of the blacksmith hammering out shoes for Master Hackler's horses.

Were the whitefolks on the riverbank following us? I wondered.

Floating logs thumped into the boat. A flickering boat lantern passed by in the middle of the river, with two men singing to themselves in the darkness. Sounded like they were both rum-drunk, and so they never saw us at all.

Slowly, our boat moved toward the shore, and not long after, the man said, "Keep still," and we scraped into a riverbank.

Had we made it all the way across the water?

Wrapping a rough hand around my arm, the man pulled me to standing. "Climb out, and be quick about it, boy," he said. "Step down right here. Hurry, now. It ain't deep."

Heart pounding, I set one foot at a time on the muddy river bottom. Behind me, Harrison climbed out. Holding on to the side of the boat to steady himself, he grabbed the tow sack, and waded into shore.

But it felt strange to stand on the Ohio riverbank and look across the water toward the Kentucky side we had left behind because, truth was, the Ohio side didn't look any different than the dark Kentucky shore.

It made me think of the time that I stole a look in Miz Catherine's mirror and jumped at seeing myself staring back from the silver glass. Looking across the River Jordan was just like staring in that mirror. One side seemed the same as the other.

"You planning on climbing out?" The river man looked back at Hetty Scott, who still sat in the boat, staring wide-eyed from the layers of clothing that surrounded her. I could count three bonnets circling her round face, and so many layers of fancy dresses and petticoats, it was hard to tell where the clothing ended and she began.

She fluttered her hands. "Can't climb out in the river."

The man spat on the riverbank. "What were you planning on doing once you got over here?" he said loudly. "Just parade around in whitefolks' clothing and shoes? Or did you figure you could steal all those fancy things from your mistress and run away like that?"

"Lordy, I just don't know," Hetty Scott said, burrowing deeper into her nest of clothes. "I just wanted some pretty things. Never had no pretty things before, you know." Her hands kept patting the big striped bonnet she wore tied around the others, as if it was the only thing she had left in the world.

I felt sorry for Hetty Scott, hearing the way the man was talking to her and knowing that we had a whole sackful of stolen things ourselves—when, quick as anything, the man reached into the rowboat, picked up his pistol, and stuck it in front of Hetty Scott's face. In his other hand, he held the knife that had been setting on his seat. Hetty Scott gasped sharp, and her hands flew like two ribbons to cover her mouth.

"You hear them coming across the water after you?" the river man said low and mean. "You leave those fancy clothes behind, or I'm gonna send you back into the river." He waved his pistol in the direction of the river. "That's the choice I'm giving you. I'm not taking a fool with me."

Hetty Scott sent up a wail then that would have awakened the dead.

"Let me keep my pretty clothes," she cried. "I'm takin my pretty clothes to CANADAY. I can't leave all my pretty clothes . . ."

Before me and Harrison could say a word, the man stuck the

pistol in his pocket, grabbed the front of the boat, and pushed it deeper into the water. Holding the side of the boat, knee-deep in the river, the man said again, "You coming with us or not? You have one-half minute to answer me. You coming or not?"

"Don't you go and take away all my pretty clothes," Hetty Scott wept. "Please let me keep ahold of my pretty clothes. I never had pretty—"

With one strong heave, the man pushed the boat away.

Me and Harrison watched like two stunned birds as the boat with poor Hetty Scott sitting inside began to make a slow, haunting turn into the river's current. Hetty Scott leaned over the side, waving her arms and wailing for us to help her. I could see her bonnets turning all which-way and one oar dragging back in the water. And even as the boat's dark shape disappeared from our sight, I could still hear her sad, crying voice echoing up the river.

Fear crawled right up my spine.

Saying nothing about what he had done to Hetty Scott, the man waded out of the water and walked right past me and Harrison. I heard the hard snap of twigs and brush as he stomped into the woods.

"Samuel," Harrison said, pointing. "Go on. We s'posed to be following him." But I didn't want to follow the man's cold shadow as it disappeared among the trees. I figured he was just gonna leave us somewhere, same as he had done to poor Hetty Scott.

A Forest of Silence

"Who else we gonna follow?" Harrison hissed. "Can't just stand on the riverbank waitin for them patrollers to come across the river and find us." Harrison started into the woods, carrying the tow sack and leaning on his walking stick. He waved his arm, telling me to hurry.

But the river man was walking fast. Holding his pistol in one hand and the knife in the other, he weaved back and forth, cutting a crooked line around trees and fallen logs. It made my legs feel like someone had set them on fire, trying to keep up. As I followed his mean back, all kinds of questions circled inside my head.

Why had he gone and done something so terrible to poor Hetty Scott when she didn't do anything wrong? Why had he brought us across the river at all? Couldn't he see us walking and walking behind him? Where was he taking me and Harrison to?

Then the man stopped so sudden in the middle of the woods, I almost jumped out of my skin.

He stared hard at me.

Had he heard the talking in my head?

"How old are you, son?"

"Eleven," I answered quiet. Kept my eyes down.

"That old man got a name?"

"Harrison. But he ain't that old," I lied. "He only got rig-or mortis in his bones from working in the fields when he was young."

"Rig-or mortis," the man gave a deep, rolling laugh. Sounded like the laugh had something mean behind it. Like summer thunder coming across the cornfields.

The man looked back at Harrison, who was hobbling so far behind that all you could see was a speck of white tow sack in the dark woods. "I traveled with an old man once," he said. "When I was eight, they chained me to an old Negro. Walked most of a hundred miles together, Norfolk to Richmond, Virginia. And I remember, plain as day, how that old, bent-over man held up most of the chain between us, trying to make those irons light as he could for me."

The river man paused and looked at me. "You know what irons are, boy?"

"No, sir."

Reaching out quick, he circled his hand around my throat. "Collars they fasten here, around your neck."

His hand tightened, and fear stuck in my throat. In a voice that I tried to keep calm as water, I asked him what he had done wrong to be put in irons.

"Wrong?" The man squeezed his hand, and my fingers flew to my throat, trying to pull his hand free. Even after he let go, it felt like something stayed circled tight around my neck.

"I was a slave boy, same as you," the man's voice rumbled. "Sold for the first time when I was eight and a half-dozen times after that." He gave me a hard look. "You never saw blackfolks put in irons and sold before?"

I thought of the picture I had of my momma. In my mind, I had always seen her riding away like a white person, sitting in a wagon. Maybe the truth was that she had been chained like the man was saying, chained around the neck like dogs are and walked all the way to Washington, Kentucky, to be sold.

"See this?" The man traced his finger down one jagged scar on his dark face. "Your master ever beat you like this?"

"No, sir," I whispered.

"Know how I got my scars?" He held out his arms, pointing to all the scars. Some jagged stripes, some round like pox marks. "You see what those marks are?"

"Smallpox?"

"Look." He held his arm closer. "They look like nail marks to you?"

My throat tightened.

"I was beaten by a board with a nail stuck through it," the man's voice kept on, low and angry. "When I wasn't much older than you. My master, he came home mad-drunk one night, tore a board off the wall, and beat me 'til the blood ran down my skin in rivers."

The man turned away. "Don't you forget what can happen to you," he said over his shoulder. "You don't watch your step, trouble'll find your black skin too." And then he walked ahead, snapping branches like bones under his feet.

A whole forest of silence grew up after his words. Seemed like the night air had pulled in its breath at hearing what the river man said. Seemed like the breath had been taken out of me too.

"Lord, Samuel!" Harrison's loud whisper made me jump. "I never thought I was gonna catch up." He leaned hard on my shoulder. "Feel like I done walked the bones clear outta my feet, how 'bout you?"

"Yes," I said, my voice sounding strange and trembly.

"That fellow say anything to you?"

I tried to remember what Lilly put in her turnover pies, and the names of each one of the hogs in Master Hackler's barn, to keep from thinking about the man's scars and what he had said.

"He tell you why he sent that poor lady into the river?"

I shook my head.

"Don't understand that atall. Why would a fellow go and do something like that? Send that poor slave lady out into the river to be caught like that? Just 'cause she was scared outta her daylights and mixed up about some fancy clothes ain't no reason to do something like that. Don't understand that atall . . ." Harrison sighed and shifted the tow sack from one shoulder to the other.

Not looking back at us, the river man followed a small creek through the woods. It twisted and turned like a piece of rope. He stayed to one side of the creek, moving through places where the ground was soft and thick with moss.

"That fellow knows where he's going to. You can just tell," Harrison whispered as we walked. "He's takin us somewhere. My legs may not hold out long 'nough to get there, but he's takin us somewhere—"

It was almost light before we stopped at a clearing where a small house and frame barn sat silent. The house was made of neat, brown bricks and made me think of a loaf of Lilly's bread. Behind it, there was a gray barn that looked the same as Master Hackler's, only this barn was straight up and Master Hackler's sagged to one side, as if it had been standing in a strong wind too long.

I noticed a yellow-painted chair sitting in the tall grass near the house. If someone had left one of Miz Catherine's chairs outside, it would have put her in a fit worse than I could imagine. My fingers itched to take the chair back into that house so someone wouldn't get themselves in trouble.

The man stopped before we got near the house. Seemed like he noticed the yellow-painted chair too, but he didn't say a word about it.

"Keep quiet and listen close, now," he said sharply, keeping his eyes fixed on the house and the woods. "Everything's all ready, it looks like. But you do exactly what I tell you, understand?" He glared at us. "I'm only gonna go through this once before I leave."

In the dim morning light, I could see the man was dog-tired. His big shoulders were slumped over like they had melted down, and the front of his shirt pressed against his skin with dark circles of sweat. River mud splattered his clothes all over.

"You walk around the back of that house until you see a white-painted cellar door standing open, with steps going down," the man said, pointing at the house. "You go and hide yourself in that cellar. Could be for a day. Could be two or three days. But there's food and blankets already down there for you. So you just wait there and keep quiet until the white widow lady who lives in the house takes you to another—"

The man cut a look at Harrison.

"You listening to what I'm saying, old man?"

But Harrison was leaning on his walking stick, head down, eyes closed. He looked as spent as I had ever seen, not even like himself anymore.

The man turned to me. His voice hissed slow and mean. "You got any sense?"

I didn't dare look up. Just nodded yes.

"Then you heard what I told the old man—you and him hide in that cellar and keep quiet until the white widow lady takes you to another safe place."

In my mind, I tried to conjure up a picture of what kind of white lady would go around helping blackfolks, but I couldn't. Lilly always said Miz Catherine would cut off her own right arm and sell her left one rather than lift a hand to help us, even if we were keeled over and dying.

The man tapped my chest with his pistol. "You gonna remember what I said in the woods? You gonna remember how I got all my scars?"

I nodded, keeping my eyes fixed on the front of his red shirt.

"There's two things I learned when I run off like you and got away from my own master." He stuck the gun in his pocket and told me to look up. Slowly, I looked at the river man's scar-ruined face, his eyes staring at me like two bottomless holes. "First," he said, "you always walk as if you have the perfect right to do so, the same as whitefolks walk. Go on, walk toward that tree—"

The river man pushed me forward. I stumbled, and then started across the clearing, walking the way I always do. He followed right behind. "Draw attention to yourself," he said, giving me another hard push. "Don't scuttle around like some poor, bent-over beetle carrying a few crumbs to his master. You slave or free? Walk like it. WALK!"

Ten times, twenty times, he made me walk back and forth between two trees. Picking up my feet. Keeping my back straight. Swinging my arms. Putting my nose in the air like I was smelling the wind.

Leaning on his walking stick, Harrison stood and watched, saying nothing.

"Wait." The man latched onto my arm and stopped me right in the middle of walking. "Say I'm a white fellow—maybe a patroller—who's caught ahold of you. What are you gonna do now, boy?"

My heart thumped in my chest. His rough hand squeezed my arm tighter. "You want to run?" he said.

"Yes" came whispering out of my mouth.

"No," the man's voice rumbled. "You run, they know exactly who you are. Haste will always be your undoing. You wait and look for their weakness. Then you plan a way out. Never go running off, understand?" He glared at me. "You have these things set down in your head or not, boy?"

I nodded. *Walk. Don't haste.*

The man glanced over at Harrison. "Go and get me that old man of yours and tell him to bring along the bundle he's been carrying."

Slow and shuffling, Harrison brought over our bundle of stolen things. "Ain't nothin much in here but food and clothes for me and Samuel," he said, keeping his eyes low. "We only run off with what belongs to us."

But the man opened up the tow sack like he owned it himself. Saw Miz Catherine's bonnet, Master Hackler's boots, and all the other things, of course. With no expression on his face at all, he tied the bundle closed.

"I'll be taking your tow sack along with me," he said, lifting it to his shoulder.

I thought about all the things inside that tow sack . . . the silver pocket watch Harrison was gonna sell for money, the bridle for the horse he thought we'd have someday, the blankets that belonged to me, the skillet from Lilly's kitchen . . .

"Wait," Harrison said.

"Something wrong, old man?" The man gave Harrison a squint look. Like Harrison was nothing more than a flyspeck or spot of dirt. Nothing that mattered much.

Harrison cleared his throat. "There's a roll of gray yarn in the bottom of that tow sack. Couldn't we keep ahold of it maybe? It belongs—" He paused and looked quick at me. "To Samuel."

Gray yarn?

I stared at Harrison. What was he talking about? Why would he ask for the gray yarn and why would it belong to me?

Even the man seemed set back a little. He looked first at Harrison, then at me. Shaking his head, he lowered the bundle to the ground, untied it, and hunted around for the roll of yarn.

"Here," he said, pulling out something and tossing it to me.

I looked down at the small tangle of wool in my hands, and the river man grinned like it was something funny to see me holding nothing but that yarn.

"Don't suppose you thought to bring any money in this sack?" he said, lifting the bundle in the air and shaking it hard. "Or were you thinking that a little roll of gray yarn was gonna buy you everything you need in this world, old man?"

Harrison was silent.

"Lucky day for you that I got some spare money to give away." The river man loosened a small leather pouch tied to his belt and nodded toward the brown house. "You pay the white widow lady for keeping you in her cellar, and other folks if they ask for money." He tossed the leather pouch to Harrison. "Remember where you put it, old man." But the pouch tumbled through Harrison's stiff fingers and jangled to the ground.

"One more thing," the river man said as he lifted the tow sack to his shoulder. "Slave catchers and patrollers, they have the right to hunt any old place they please. They can come across the river and catch you here in Ohio, the same as Kentucky. You understand what I'm saying?"

Harrison nodded.

"There's nowhere in this whole United States that a runaway is safe," the river man called over his shoulder. "You just remember that."

And without another word, he turned and walked into the woods, his legs cutting up the ground like a big pair of saw blades. The last I saw was his red-flannel back carrying all our things, disappearing between the trees.

Me and Harrison hurried toward the house, just as a rooster crowed.

The Gray Yarn

The white doors of the cellar stood open as if expecting us.

Four old stoneware crocks sat on the steps going down. They looked like they were filled with nothing except rainwater and cobwebs. But as we stepped past them, a brown field mouse suddenly darted out from the shadows, and we nearly jumped out of our skin.

Telling me to wait until he had a look around, Harrison ducked his head and crept into the cellar first. Then his hand poked out of the darkness and waved for me to follow.

It took my eyes a while to see into the shadows. The cellar was a low, squarish room. Half-cut tree logs, with the bark still on them, ran close over our heads, and the floor was hard-packed clay, same as Master Hackler's.

Beside me, Harrison whispered, "You see anything, Samuel? I can't see a thing down here in all this mess. How 'bout you? You see something for us?"

About a hundred and one things were scattered and stuffed into the cellar. It would have put Lilly in a fit, the way things were left all which-way. Carpenter's tools, a half-made chest, and two small red-painted cupboards lay at the foot of the steps, as if the fellow making them had just set them there, turned, and run off. Deeper in the shadows, I could see big

95

wooden barrels, the half-moon shape of buggy wheels, sacks of potatoes or turnips, a pile of broken chairs, and a heap of other things against the walls.

"Go on over there," Harrison whispered, pointing at the far end of the cellar. "Just poke around a little."

At the other end of the room, my eyes caught sight of something. Hidden behind a wall of barrels stacked almost to the ceiling beams was a ragged corner of blue and white. Coming around, I saw an old straw pallet and a pile of coverlets setting there, plain as day, with a crock of buttermilk, a brown jug of cider, and a basket stuffed full of food beside them.

"Harrison!" I called out. "Look here."

"What?" Harrison said, stumbling and climbing through the dark cellar. "What?" When he got to where I was standing and looked around the row of barrels, he squeezed his eyes shut and raised his hands up toward the ceiling.

"Glor-ee be. Glor-ee be. Glor-ee be," he whispered, shaking his hands in the air. "That man was telling the truth, sure enough, he was."

After that, me and Harrison pounced on the food faster than two half-starved cats on the back of a bird. We hadn't eaten at all since we had been in the cornfield, the day before. So we snapped up the pieces of bread sopped in buttermilk, the jelly cup, the slice of cold bacon at the bottom of the basket, and the caved-in baked apple. I was so awful thirsty, I gulped down more than half of the jug of cider, and Harrison had to tug it out of my hands to get some for himself.

"You is spoiled to a stink, Samuel." He grinned, shaking his head. "Gimme some of that cider now."

But after we had eaten everything that had been left in our hiding place, down to the dried-up crumbs in the bottom of the basket, I was still hungry as a horse, and I got the idea of poking around the cellar for more food and cider.

Only, Harrison wouldn't even hear of it.

"That ain't the right thing to do, stealin," Harrison said, leaning back against the cellar wall and pulling a blanket up to his chin. "You ate plenty enough. Don't wanta hear no more about it, Samuel."

"But you stole from Mas Hackler," I said, my voice rising. "You took the boots, and the gloves, and the fancy bonnet from Miz—"

"You hush," Harrison said, glaring at me. "That weren't stealin." He looked up at the wood planks over our heads. "Now, you be quiet. Folks is livin up there, you hear?"

But still I kept on.

"Why is me stealin more food wrong and what you done ain't?"

Harrison pressed his lips together in one angry line. " 'Cause stealin is takin things that don't belong to you, and I didn't take nothing that didn't belong to me."

He held his hands out, palms up. "Look at these ol' hands of mine." His stiff fingers trembled. "Who owns these hands?"

"You does."

"Samuel." He squinted hard at me. "You got anything sittin on them shoulders that thinks or not?" He smacked his left hand. "Who OWNS this hand? Who BOUGHT this hand?"

"Mas Hackler?" I tried.

"An' who owns this leg?"

"Mas Hackler."

He kept going on and on, pointing to his arms, and his legs, and his back, and his feet, and then my feet, and my arms, and my legs—making me say Master Hackler's name each time—until I wished I hadn't even breathed a word in the first place.

And then Harrison said, "Now, if my hands don't belong to me and they take something that don't belong to me neither, is that stealin?"

"I s'pose not," I said uneasily, because Harrison wasn't making one bit of sense.

"All right, then." Harrison leaned back against the wall and closed his eyes. "That's why what I done wasn't wrong."

I thought for a while. Then I asked real low and quiet, "So you sayin it ain't wrong if I take more things to eat and drink from the cellar, 'cause my hands don't belong to me?"

Harrison's eyes flashed open and he snapped, "Was you listenin atall, Samuel? This cellar don't BELONG to us, and our hands don't BELONG to Mas'er Hackler no more, so if we take something from this cellar, THAT would be stealin." He unfolded another one of the blankets, and tucked it around him. "Lordy, you is thick as a turnip sometimes."

I was getting more and more angry. Harrison was talking nonsense about what was stealing and what wasn't, and what belonged to us and what didn't, and I was hungry, hungrier than all the times Master Hackler or Miz Catherine had taken away my supper meals, and a whole cellar full of good food was sitting around us—

My eyes fell on the roll of gray yarn setting beside the empty basket.

"This yarn belong to me?" I said, holding up the gray yarn and waving it in front of Harrison. "You said it did before."

"Yes." Harrison looked down at his hands.

"Then I'm gonna give away my gray yarn for takin some more food. Say I leave the yarn right here—" I stood up and set it carefully on the top of one of the barrels. "So whoever comes down in the cellar can find it. And then taking more food for my ownself ain't wrong."

Harrison sighed. "You can't give away that gray yarn, Samuel."

"I'm hungry." I stared hard at Harrison. My breath went in and out, in fast and angry puffs. "I don't want no worthless ol' piece of yarn."

"It ain't worthless," Harrison said softly.

"Looks worthless to me." I picked up the yarn and pulled at the tangles.

"Well, you doesn't know everything, does you?" Harrison answered sharply. He laid down, smacked a place for his head in the straw tick, and turned his face to the wall.

"Yes, I does."

Harrison was silent.

"Yes, I does," I said louder.

"Then you sho' must know where that gray yarn come from." Harrison's voice was muffled by the blankets.

"Where?" My voice was sharp and angry. "Where'd it come from?"

Harrison's head turned to look at me.

"Your own momma," he snapped.

I stared at Harrison. It seemed like the threads grew warm in my hand after he said that. Almost as if my momma herself had just given the yarn to me right there.

Used to be, I would ask Lilly if my momma had used this rolling pin or that flatiron, just to set my hands on something that she had touched, since there was nothing left for remembering her. But, in all the time they had raised me, Lilly and Harrison had never said one word about having gray yarn that once belonged to my momma. They had never told me about anything she had left behind when she was sold off—

"Stop thinkin up a hundred and one questions to be asking," Harrison said sharply. "I ain't talkin no more about it." He smacked the straw tick with his hand. "Now, you lay down here and git some sleep, or I'm gonna hand you over to them dogs my ownself. I'm powerful tired of you."

Heaving a loud sigh, I lay down on the smallest edge of the straw tick, as far away as I could get from old Harrison. I put the yarn right in front of me where I could see it. Maybe I figured that looking at it would remind me of something about my momma. Squinting my eyes, I tried to see her hands spinning the wool. Did she have thin, skinny-bone fingers like mine? Was she gonna use the yarn for making something? Maybe something for me?

Then a terrible thought went through my mind.

Did they take her right in the middle of her work? Was she spinning the same yarn Harrison had given to me?

My mouth turned dry as dust, thinking about it.

"Harrison," I turned my head and whispered real quiet. "Harrison, you there?"

But Harrison was breathing slow and even like he was in a deep sleep. If I woke him, I knew he would be in a fit worse than one of Miz Catherine's. So I set my head back down, closed my eyes, and tried to think of something else besides my momma spinning that yarn.

And I must have fallen asleep after that because the next thing I knew, Harrison was shaking me awake and quick footsteps were coming down the steps and across the cellar floor.

Widow Taylor

The footsteps stopped on the other side of the wall of barrels, and a white woman's voice spoke up, fast and breathless.

"I'm Mrs. Lucy Taylor," the voice said. "And I have my husband's rifle with me and I know how to use it because he taught me and I'm not afraid to shoot anything, even colored people, so . . ." The voice slowed and paused, as if thinking what to say. "So . . ." There was a long silence. "So you best not cause me any kind of trouble," the voice finished quickly.

Beside me, Harrison sat up fast.

His hands plucked at his coat, the blankets, and the basket, looking for something. "We got money to pay you, Miz Taylor," he called out. "That fellow in the boat give us money to pay you. Lord, have mercy, don't shoot us. Me and Samuel, we'll go and give you all the money we got."

Shaking the leather pouch, Harrison poured the coins into his trembling hand. One rolled silently into the blankets. "Go on, git that coin, Samuel," he whispered.

"How many coloreds are hiding behind the barrels? I hear two of you. Are there more?"

"That's all. Just an old man and a boy," Harrison said.

"Come out from behind the barrels so I can see you."

My heart hammered in my ears as me and Harrison moved out from where we were hiding like two caught mice.

On the other side stood the woman who called herself Lucy Taylor. She was smaller than her voice sounded, and dressed head to toe in black. Black bonnet. Black dress. Black shoes. An old hunting rifle rested against the silk folds of her dress, and her face was shadowed in the deep black bonnet.

The widow lady, I thought. That's who this is.

But glancing quick at her hands, I noticed a strange thing. The white hands wrapped around the rifle weren't the wrinkled and thin-skinned hands of an old widow lady. They were smooth and young.

"You don't need to come any closer," the woman said. "Just stand there."

Me and Harrison stopped in our footsteps, not saying a word.

"Did you come a long way?" the woman asked after an uncomfortable-long silence. She stared at us, holding that gunmetal tight.

"Aways," Harrison answered, keeping his eyes down. "Yes'm."

"Is the boy someone's slave too?"

Harrison's hand tightened on my arm. "Yes'm."

I could hear the woman's dress rustling as she stepped closer and peered at me from her black bonnet. She had a round, pale face, and the way it looked inside her bonnet made me think of a spring bulb set inside the earth. "My family in Kentucky kept slaves. A colored woman looked after me, growing up. Her name was Letty." She turned to Harrison. "Did you ever know a colored woman named Letty?"

"No'm." Harrison cleared his throat. "But we got money here to pay you, if you just let us go on now. We ain't gonna cause you no more trouble." He held out his handful of silver coins. "Just let me and Samuel move on to another place."

The woman was silent, not even looking at the coins. Then she said real quiet and sudden, "My husband, Jacob, is dead."

Harrison looked down. "Purely sorry to hear that."

"He came down with a fever in August after that spell of hot weather we had," the woman said in a tight-strung voice. "The doctor in town tried all of his fancy remedies. Jacob is as strong as a horse, he told me. But I came into Jacob's bedchamber one morning, and he opened his eyes and told me that he was going away. By that evening he was dead."

"Purely sorry to hear that," Harrison said again.

There was more silence, and then the woman said softly, "I have seen him, though." Eyes wide, she looked at Harrison. "Do colored people believe in seeing those who are gone?"

A shiver went through me, but Harrison cleared his throat and said slowly, "Well, now, I s'pose, yes'm, I s'pose they does."

The Widow Taylor ducked her bonnet down. "I see Jacob in the kitchen sometimes," she said quietly. "He sits at the table, looking the same as he did in life, and he tells me how to do things when I am close to tears . . . how to figure the farm accounts and how to pull corn for fodder and how to prime the pump for his well. He says—"

The woman's voice trembled and stopped, and she reached for something behind her. "Well, now, it's almost evening. Here, I brought you some supper," she said in a hurry. "You have been sleeping in the cellar all day without any food to eat."

She set a basket of food on the floor in front of her. "I put in a ham bone left from yesterday's stew, and six corn cakes, and a handful of snap beans," she said, tapping the basket with her foot. "Tomorrow evening, what I will do is drive Jacob's wagon around to the cellar door and take you to Reverend Pry's church when I go for my ladies' prayer meeting. Reverend Pry's church is where Jacob always took the coloreds next."

She stared at me and Harrison with a scared kind of look in her eyes again. "You won't give me any difficulties this evening or tomorrow, will you? You won't take any of Jacob's things from the cellar and run off, will you?"

Harrison held out the coins again. "Me and Samuel got plenty of money to pay you for all that food, Miz Taylor."

"Yes, well . . ." Her voice trembled. "I suppose . . ."

I watched as the widow lady opened a black-edged handkerchief and set it carefully on the clay floor between us. "Put five of your coins there," she said, keeping her eyes on us.

Harrison reached down and dropped five silver coins into the middle of the handkerchief.

"You can step away now," the lady said, and after we moved far enough back, she bent over and lifted each lace corner of the handkerchief real careful-like, so that her white fingers didn't touch the same coins that our black hands had touched. Miz Catherine was always that way, too. Made me feel like my skin was no different than fireplace soot.

Miz Taylor tucked the handkerchief in her dress and picked up the hunting rifle. "I didn't want to keep on hiding colored people in the cellar," she said, turning to leave. "But Jacob told me to carry his rifle and to keep doing the things just the same as he would do. You'll tell me if you see him down here, won't you?"

Then, in a swirl of black silk, she ran up the steps and shut the cellar doors behind her, leaving me and Harrison in the pitch darkness.

"Lord, have mercy," Harrison said loudly. "You still standin next to me, Samuel?" He reached out and clapped a hand on my shoulder.

Squinting into the shadows, I said, "You don't think her dead husband is up and walking round here, do you? Like she said he was?"

"Lordy, I sure do hope not. Last thing I need to worry about is dead whitefolks too." Harrison shuffled forward. "Now, where'd she go and leave that good basket of food?"

Sitting down on the straw tick, we divided up the food she

had brought. Harrison left most of the ham bone and four corn cakes for me, and took just two little corn cakes and a few snap beans for himself.

"Ain't that hungry," he said, but I figured he was remembering how I had been begging and scraping for some more food that morning.

While we were eating those corn cakes, I started thinking about the gray yarn again, and I tried asking about it, thinking maybe Harrison would tell me something more. "This gray yarn come from my momma?" I said, picking up the tangle of wool.

"Yes." Harrison nodded his head and chewed slow and silent. "And you already heard all you needs to know, Samuel."

But I kept on.

"Was my momma spinning this yarn when Mas Hackler took her away?"

Harrison fixed me with a stare.

"That why you kept it? 'Cause of that?"

Harrison heaved a loud, angry sigh. "Samuel, you try my soul worse than the Devil himself. I ain't tellin you anything else, you hear?" His voice rose. "I got good enough reasons for keeping some things secret, and if you keep on askin me foolish things, I swear I will just up and leave, you hear?"

He snapped his handful of beans hard.

Snap, snap, snap.

I put the yarn in my pocket and kept quiet. "Don't you feel sorry for that white lady, being left alone like that?" I asked. "I feel sorry for her missing her husband so much. She ain't very old."

"Well," Harrison said, still sounding mad, "I don't."

"Why?" I picked at the ham bone.

" 'Cause corn and crows don't grow in the same field."

"What?"

"Whitefolks and blackfolks ain't got the same feelings. They ain't the same people as us. I don't know how whitefolks feel, and they sure don't know one sorry thing about me. Corn and crows, they don't grow in the same field."

"You sayin you ain't sad when someone up and dies?"

I thought about Lilly going to visit her children in the Negro burying-ground and talking to each one of them. "Now, Viney," she'd say to the one. "Don't you go tearing 'round heaven all the time, like you used to when you was down here with us . . ."

"If they's white, I got one feeling. If they's black, I got another," Harrison said.

I stared at Harrison, my mouth open.

"You sayin you feel HAPPY when whitefolks die?"

Harrison smacked my arm. "Course not. You want me to go straight to hell right now, Samuel? Lord Almighty, what makes you talk like that?" He brushed cornbread crumbs off his shirt. "I'm just sayin that I got enough things of my own to feel sorry about, and a white lady and her dead husband who I never met before ain't something I feel sorry about. If I died right here, you think she'd feel pity for my ol' black skin? You figure she'd raise one finger to help you?"

I thought about how she had picked up the coins in the handkerchief, corner by corner. "I don't know," I told Harrison. "Maybe."

"No maybe 'bout it," Harrison snorted. "You a fool if you think so."

But later that night, after Harrison had fallen asleep, I heard the white lady crying to herself, and I am ashamed to say that I felt downright sorry for her. The sound came from a room above the cellar, maybe a bedchamber, and the terrible-sad wailing almost set me crying too. I heard the lady calling out the name Jacob Taylor, over and over, and talking to no one about the farm and the doctor and the church, and I felt sorry enough to have gone up the steps myself and fetched a cold rag for her poor lost senses.

I thought that this side of the River Jordan would be better than the side we had come from. From what Harrison had told me, I figured that all of the blackfolks over here would be free, and all of the mean whitefolks and dogs would be gone, left behind. But this side of the river was full of its own kind of trouble, seemed like.

I pictured the ghost of Jacob Taylor floating around, and a

shiver went clear through me. Was he keeping his eye on me and Harrison? Was he making sure we didn't run off?

Something tumbled over in the cellar. Maybe it was a mouse skittering around, but I couldn't wait for another day to come, so that we could climb into the wagon and leave the Widow Taylor's sad house behind.

Beneath Hay and Feed Sacks

The next evening, the Widow Taylor came around to the cellar door. We heard the creaking of the wagon wheels, and her voice talking to the horse. "Now, Jupe, you listen to me. Move up, Jupe. You are not going over there. You stop right here. Whoa, Jupe." The horse snorted loudly outside. "Don't toss your head at me, old fellow," she scolded. "Because I won't stand for it."

The cellar door opened. "Come out of there now," the Widow Taylor called to us sharply. "I'm here with the wagon."

Me and Harrison were already waiting for her. I had spent the whole day going up and down the steps every little while to see if sunlight was still shining through the cracks around the cellar door.

"Ain't it dark yet?" Harrison kept asking. "Where you think that white lady is?"

His rigor mortis had set in again, so most of the afternoon, he had stayed piled up in the coverlets, and twice he had me poke around the cellar, looking for an old ax to put under the straw tick so he could keep the chills away.

But finally, the Widow Taylor had come with the wagon.

Me and Harrison left that cellar fast. After two days in the darkness, we hurried up the steps and stood outside, trying to get our eyes used to seeing in the light. The sun was setting just below the far trees, and the air smelled of wood smoke and warm earth. I breathed in a whole lungful of that good air, as if I had never taken a living breath before.

"Over here," the Widow Taylor said impatiently. She stood at the front of an old-looking brown horse, with her fingers curled around his bridle. His head swung up and down, blowing a snort of air.

"You be still, Jupe." She gave him a soft slap on the neck. "He doesn't like coloreds much, you can tell," she said.

But in my mind I thought maybe, truth was, he didn't like the Widow Taylor much, because she was the one holding tight to his bridle, not us.

"Climb in," she said, pointing at the wagon. "Jacob always puts the coloreds in the back underneath the hay and feed sacks. Just be careful of his good things."

I don't know what the lady meant about Jacob's good things. The wagon was a mess of tools, barrels, cordwood, and clumps of dirty hay, just like the cellar. There was nothing fancy or nice at all.

"You go on and hide yourself right here," Harrison whispered, shaking out a pile of old tow sacks. Shriveled-up brown apples rolled everywhere. "I'm gonna hide myself under that pile of hay." He leaned closer. "Anything happens, if we git stopped along the way, you just stay covered up right where you is, and you don't breathe a word. You let Harrison do whatever needs done, you understand?"

The Widow Taylor came over to the side of the wagon.

"I'm ready to leave," she said loudly. "It's getting late."

"All right, yes'm, I'm hurryin," Harrison said. "Go on, git underneath these feed sacks, Samuel." He lifted the sacks and gave me a hard stare, and there wasn't a thing I could do but crawl under the scratchy pile that smelled of earth and rotted apples.

"The ladies have a prayer meeting and hymn-sing every Thursday evening at Reverend Pry's church," the widow lady told Harrison. "Last week Jacob rode in the wagon and watched over Jupe until we had finished our meeting. He told me everything sounded so sweet and nice."

A shiver went through me, hearing the way the Widow Taylor kept talking so real about her dead husband.

"Did you see Jacob while you were down in the cellar last night?" she asked Harrison. "Did he talk to you?"

"Well, now," Harrison said, coughing, "we didn't, no, but we been sleepin pretty sound."

"I talked to Jacob last night, and he said he was going to have a look at you. I said you were an old colored man with a young boy. Are you certain that you didn't speak to him?"

I recollected how she had cried and sobbed the night before, and there weren't any other voices, not Jacob's or any others.

"Could be that we did," Harrison answered uneasily.

"My husband is a good man, isn't he?"

"Yes'm," came Harrison's muffled reply. "That's the truth."

"Now, once we get to Reverend Pry's church, all you will

need to do is climb out of the wagon after our hymn singing starts and go around to the side door of the church, the one next to the big currant bush. Do you know what currants are?"

"Yes'm," Harrison answered again, and I thought about the big currant bush that grew in the back of Lilly's cabin, full of sour red-black berries. "Ain't that the picture of life?" Lilly used to chuckle every time we walked by it. "Good-looking berries that be sour and stuck with thorns."

Miz Taylor kept rattling on. "Well, you and the boy will have to sneak through the church door by those currant bushes, and after that, Reverend Pry will find you and he'll take good care of you. He's saved dozens of coloreds." There was a pause, and the wagon creaked as if the widow lady was climbing up to her seat. I heard the sound of the reins being loosened and untangled. "Ready, then?" she asked Harrison.

I didn't hear Harrison's answer, but the wagon jolted forward after that, and we were on our way. I curled my fingers around my momma's gray yarn in my pocket.

Strange to say, I had never seen a real church before.

Our Poor Colored Brethren

The Widow Taylor talked up a storm of nonsense to her dead husband, all the way to the church. Even hidden underneath the feed sacks, I could hear her talking.

"Jacob," she said, stopping the wagon suddenly. "Climb down and see if that is a snake curled up in the road, would you please." And another time, when the wagon wheel stuck fast in a rut, she said, "Jacob, would you be so kind as to put a rail under that left wheel." But I heard her heave a sigh, climb down from the wagon seat, and put a plank under that wheel herself.

With all the stopping and starting and getting stuck, it seemed like the road we took was more than a week long. Underneath the feed sacks, my skin itched, and I could hardly breathe from the smell of those spoiled apples. When we stopped for the last time, it was nearly dark outside. Harrison crawled over and lifted up the feed sacks. "Git a-movin, Samuel," he whispered.

In front of the wagon, I saw a good-sized building made of white bricks. Looked just like little blocks of salt, set one on top of the other, right to the night sky. Three skinny-long windows faced out into the dusk, and there were candles flickering on the panes. From one open window, the sound of thin, unsteady singing drifted out.

"Hurry, Samuel," Harrison said sharply. "That widow lady's already gone inside."

But it was a strange feeling to climb out of the wagon and creep up to that fancy whitefolks' church. Me and Harrison moved along the side of Miz Taylor's wagon and horse, then along the side of another wagon, keeping low. The horses tied in the yard moved and nickered uneasily. Wagon trace chains jangled in the darkness, and I had the suspicion that when we got to the door of the church a whole group of white patrollers would jump out of the shadows, and the church building would crumble to nothing more than a pile of salt at our feet.

But the only thing that happened was that Harrison couldn't get the side door open. It was stuck closed.

"Well, now—" Harrison looked up at the night sky and then out at the yard full of wagons and horses. "That mean go in or stay out?" He shook his head. "Lord ain't sayin much this evenin, is he, Samuel?"

Putting his shoulder against the door, Harrison gave it one last shove. But this time, it swung open so suddenly, it nearly sent both of us sprawling.

We were in a small room. By the looks of it, the room belonged to a rich white fellow because it was full of fancy things. On a shiny wood table nearby, I could see books, quills, and papers scattered in the light of two oil lamps. Me and Harrison ducked down quick behind that table, fearing we had made enough noise to awaken the dead.

116

But the room stayed empty. No one came barreling in after us.

Harrison straightened up slowly and shook his head. "Lordy, Lordy," he sighed.

On the table, something caught my eye.

A powerful-big book sat in the middle like a split-open piece of a tree trunk. I leaned over to look at it. Words filled one whole side of the page, thick as weeds, and on the other side was an ink drawing so real it seemed as if it would come alive. The drawing showed two whitefolks with wings flying over an old man with a long beard. His eyes stared up at them in a frightened way, and the flying whitefolks reached out of the sky toward him. Their hands looked like such soft human hands that I had to touch the page to make sure they weren't.

"Never seen a book the size of that before," Harrison whispered, coming over. "Looks like something sent straight from the Lord himself."

"That a whitefolks' Bible?" I asked Harrison.

"Could be. Looks that way."

I trailed my fingers down the page of words.

"Nothin like Lilly's Bible," I said.

"Course not," Harrison snorted. "Whitefolks, they got their fancy big Bible. We got ours."

On the other side of the wall, the ladies' thin voices kept on singing. Harrison grinned. "Sound like a fiddle on its last string. And even that little string ain't in tune, sho' enough it ain't." He slapped his leg and shook his head back and forth in silent laughter.

The poor singing trailed off after that, and there was the sound of the church ladies making their way out of the church. Me and Harrison hunched down behind the table and listened to all the footsteps. Quick footsteps. Shuffling footsteps. Starting and stopping footsteps. After the footsteps died away, the door of our room swung open.

"Blessed are those who fear the Lord," a loud voice said, and when I raised my eyes above the table, I half-expected to see the Lord himself standing there with robes and wings just like that Bible picture. But what I saw instead was a short, white-haired man standing in the doorway with an odd-looking younger fellow.

"I'm Reverend Pry," the old man said, moving toward us with quick, cricket steps. "Welcome, my poor colored brethren."

The Reverend pointed to the other fellow. "And this is my student, Mr. Keepheart. Don't be timid about this, Mr. Keepheart. Come forward."

Mr. Keepheart was as skinny as a broomstraw, with buck-teeth the size of Seth's dominoes. But it seemed to me that the teeth smiled in a friendly way at us.

The Reverend peered at me over his spectacles. "I imagine that you must be Samuel, the Negro boy who ran away from your owner in Blue Ash, Kentucky, last Saturday evening."

The skin on my neck prickled. How did he know my name and where we had run off from?

"And," he turned to Harrison, "you must be Old Harrison, about seventy years of age, and very lame and slow, his master says—"

The Reverend's sharp black eyes stared at us, unblinking. "Is that who you both are? Am I correct?"

Harrison didn't say a word.

My heart hammered in my ears.

"I expect honesty in all things. There is no room for the dishonest man in the Lord's house." The Reverend rapped his knuckles on the table. "Speak up."

"Yes," Harrison answered low and mumbling. "Me and Samuel, that's us."

"The Lord rewards the honest man and strikes down all others," the Reverend said, sitting down at the table and picking up a quill. "Remember that."

The room was quiet. Standing there, I didn't know what to do. I didn't know what to think about strangers who knew things about us that we hadn't even said. Had we been caught?

Harrison cleared his throat. "How come you know our names? Someone been going round asking for us?"

Reverend Pry sharpened the end of his quill with a pen-knife. "There were three Kentucky folks in town yesterday afternoon, on the trail of their runaway slaves," he said, without looking up. "Mr. Keepheart talked to an older, dark-haired gentleman with two sons. One was a strapping, big fellow, and the other one was redhaired and young—"

My throat tightened. Cassius and Seth.

"They were placing notices about the escape of their old man and boy in the newspaper and such." The Reverend held his quill to the light. "Their name was Hackler, Mr. Keepheart heard them say."

Harrison jumped in. "They still here?" He looked, wild-eyed, around the room. "You seen them today?"

Mr. Keepheart shook his head no, and Reverend Pry sniffed and peered at Harrison over the top of his spectacles. "There is nothing to fear in the Lord's house," he said. "The Lord always shields the persecuted."

But the Reverend didn't know Master Hackler. He was something to fear, persecuted or not. He and Cassius both. When one of the hunting dogs had run off, he had tracked it all the way to the next town. He was the kind who would turn over every rock until he found what he was looking for.

"Come closer, Samuel." The Reverend turned up his lamp until the flame flickered out of the top. "Tell me your age."

Harrison reached out and wrapped his hand tight around my arm. "Samuel's eleven years. Come spring, he's gonna be twelve."

"Samuel. Eleven years of age," the Reverend repeated. With

his quill pen, he made marks on a piece of paper. Looked just like a long line of spiderwebs.

"Does he have a mother?" the Reverend asked Harrison, as if I didn't have any voice left to talk.

Harrison shook his head. "Sold off."

The Reverend clicked his tongue and gave Mr. Keepheart a look. "Poor young fellow," he said, and his pen scratched across the paper. Then he told me to step closer, and he gave me a long, silent stare.

I was afraid he could see every thought in my head . . . how he had the skinniest white nose I had ever seen . . . how his bristly eyebrows looked like two rolls of cotton stuck above his eyes . . . how I didn't like being in the strange whitefolks' church at all . . . how I wanted him and Mr. Keepheart to go on and leave us be . . .

The Reverend leaned over his paper, and his ink pen scratched words all over. Scratch, scratch, scratch. Sounded like hens in a chicken yard. I was sure he was writing down all my bad thoughts, one after the other, and I couldn't keep still any longer.

"What you writin down on that paper?" I said.

Setting the pen in the inkwell, the Reverend said, "I'm just putting down a little story for my congregation."

And then he picked up the paper and read, clear as anything.

"Our forty-fifth visitor was a boy named Samuel, eleven years of age. Light chestnut-colored skin, features good, wide-awake, well made, but he speaks little, the way children in bondage are apt to do. Samuel ran away from a Kentucky master who caused him to suffer severely by selling off the boy's own mother when he was only a small child. He appears of good moral character and traveled north with an aged slave named Harrison . . ."

It felt awful strange listening to the Reverend tell a story about me as if I wasn't even standing there, saying "Samuel this and Samuel that . . ." as if he had raised me the same as Harrison and Lilly had done.

Truth is, no one had ever written one word in ink about me before. Whitefolks did their writing about whitefolks, and black-folks didn't have any use for writing. So I didn't see why a reverend would bother to write a straw about me. All the same, it made me feel like I had turned into a whitefolk and grown about two feet, to hear him go on and on like that.

But Harrison's hand pulled me back, hard, out of the Reverend's lamplight. "Why you writing that about Samuel? We don't read none at all," he said, cutting his eyes at the Reverend and Mr. Keepheart.

The Reverend straightened his spectacles and tugged on the black cravat around his neck, as if it had grown too tight. "As I told the boy, I write the stories for my congregation."

"Don't believe a word of that." Harrison shook his head.

"No, I don't. No whitefolks in their right minds want to hear the story of us poor colored folks, no, sir, they don't."

"But they do."

All of us turned to Mr. Keepheart, who had finally spoken a word.

"The Reverend tells them about the trials and despair they are rescuing our poor colored brethren from, and the members of our congregation, even some who are the sons and daughters of slave-owning families in the South, are brought down to tears."

Harrison pressed his lips together. "Don't make one bit of sense to me."

"They see the humanity"—the Reverend waved his quill in the air, and drops of ink splattered on the table—"in poor colored brethren like yourselves. I tell my congregation that the Lord worketh his will in all things, and if we do such acts of benevolence to the poorest of us, we do them to the greatest . . ."

I had never heard anyone rattle on the way Reverend Pry did. Made no sense at all the way he talked, using the strangest words I'd ever heard, while waving his arms around like those whitefolks flying away in his Bible. Still, I figured that whatever he was writing down on his paper wasn't meant to bring any trouble, because Mr. Keepheart kept smiling and nodding, even though Reverend Pry didn't let him get more than a word in.

Harrison gave the Reverend a long look, like he was thinking things over, too. Then he pulled a chair close to the table and said, "Say you write something down on that paper"—he tapped the paper with his finger—" 'bout me."

But Reverend Pry pushed back his chair and stood up. "I am afraid that the hour is late and I have other matters to attend to. I will leave you in the capable care of Mr. Keepheart. He writes with a good hand and will see to your needs this evening." And without another word, the Reverend put on his coat and skittered out the door.

After the Reverend left, Mr. Keepheart sat down in front of us. I noticed he had bread crumbs stuck all to the front of his shirt, and the sleeves of his worn coat reached barely past his elbows.

"Pleased to meet you." He nodded and smiled his domino-tooth grin at Harrison. "Don't mind if I ask you a few questions—"

But then he went and asked Harrison about a hundred and one things, it seemed like.

How many masters did he have in his life? What were they like? Had his masters let him attend a church from time to time? Was he treated well or roughly? Was he fed proper meals and given good clothes and boots for winter? Did he ever get beaten or cowhided?

It seemed downright curious to me that Reverend Pry's congregation would be so interested in the life of blackfolks. Master Hackler and Miz Catherine would have fallen down in a fit if they knew Mr. Keepheart wrote down a whole page of words about Harrison. He even asked if he could have a look at the scars on his back.

"They ain't some picture to look at," Harrison said, pressing his lips together and giving Mr. Keepheart a stare. "But I could show you what they's like, I s'pose." Standing up, he took off his coat and lifted up his shirt so Mr. Keepheart could see them. I kept my eyes fixed on the table and listened to the fellow whisper, "What a terrible, terrible sight—"

But then I heard Harrison say, calm as anything, "Now, let me have a look at your back, Mr. Keepheart."

Laid to Rest

Mr. Keepheart's back was plucked-chicken white, and you could count just about every one of his ribs. His face also turned red as beets.

"There's nothing there," Mr. Keepheart said as he slowly took off his old coat and lifted his shirt. "I've never been beaten like, like, like"—he reddened—"well, I'm sorry, like some of our, well, colored brethren are. It's a terrible thing what they do where you come from, yes, well, it is . . ." he stuttered and stumbled.

"You never been beaten same as a cow or a horse or dog?" Harrison said, his eyes snapping like fire. "Never been cowhided for fishin at night 'cause you was hungry? Or lashed thirty-nine times for runnin off from your master?"

"No, well, no." Mr. Keepheart sat down and stared at the table.

"Well, then." Harrison leaned forward and jabbed his finger at the paper. "Say you write on that fancy paper of yours how my back was all cut up by scars and say you tell your congregation people about them, they won't know what them lashes on my back feels like, 'less they got them themselves, now will they?"

Mr. Keepheart said he supposed that was true. He stuck his pen in the middle of the inkwell and said he wouldn't try to write anymore that night.

I felt bad seeing how Harrison had made Mr. Keepheart, who seemed like a good-natured fellow, turn red as beets. Lilly always said that no matter what whitefolks did to me, I was to talk polite. So I told Mr. Keepheart that I wanted to hear what he had written down on his paper.

But Harrison was stubborn as an old stump.

"Don't need to hear what Mr. Keepheart wrote," he said sharply. "I knows what I look like, I knows where I come from, and I knows what I been through. I got it all in my head, and I don't need no whitefolks to tell me what they got written down in words I can't read atall. You just leave it be, Samuel. He ain't writin no more about us."

Harrison cast his eyes around the room. "Where's me and Samuel s'posed to sleep 'round here?" he asked Mr. Keepheart.

"Of course," Mr. Keepheart said, standing up so quickly he had to catch hold of his chair. "It's getting late. I'll show you."

I could hardly believe my eyes when he took us through the door into the whitefolks' church room itself. It was as big as Master Hackler's barn inside. Mr. Keepheart lifted up the oil lamp so we could admire all the white-painted benches for the congregation and the fancy red-green-and-yellow-striped carpets.

"Look up," Mr. Keepheart said, pointing.

Above our heads, a big iron lamp hung from the ceiling. Made me think of a black spider turned over on its back, holding white candles with each of its legs.

"Under that chandelier," Mr. Keepheart said in a solemn voice, "is where one poor, little runaway child was laid to rest."

I felt my heart leap into my throat.

"She came to Reverend Pry in the arms of her mother. Poor soul. She was only a baby and already too near death to be saved. So Reverend Pry saw to it that the little colored child was given a proper burial. She was buried here." Mr. Keepheart tapped on the floor with his foot. "Right where you are standing. Below the church, but in its care forever."

Me and Harrison were silent as stones, just staring down at our feet.

Lord, I said in my mind, *it's awful nice to be inside this fancy whitefolks' church room, but I don't want to be in its care forever.*

Mr. Keepheart gave a nervous kind of cough.

"Well, now," he said, "I didn't mean for that to worry you. I just thought, well, you might want to know, well, about other colored breth . . ." His freckled face reddened again. "Let me get a few blankets."

Taking the lamp, he hurried back to Reverend Pry's room and returned with an armful of old quilts and a half-eaten loaf of bread.

"You can sleep here." Mr. Keepheart piled the quilts on one of the church benches. "And I brought some leftover bread if you are feeling hungry. And here," he said, pressing a piece of barley candy into my hand. "A little something for you, Samuel. I thought perhaps you might like that."

Harrison sat down and heaved a loud sigh. "Good. You can leave us be for the night, Mr. Keepheart."

"Yes, all right, sleep well, both of you, God bless you," Mr. Keepheart stuttered and turned to leave. But at the door of the church, he turned back, lifted up the flickering lamp, and gave us a wide grin. "And don't worry, Reverend Pry won't be preaching here until Sunday," he said. "Although I have heard some folks say they sleep better when he's preaching than at most other times."

Chuckling to himself, Mr. Keepheart closed the door.

It was a strange feeling to be left in the middle of a dark and silent whitefolks' church. I heard Harrison get up from where he was sitting. He started to shuffle down the rows, between the benches.

"Where you goin to?" I spoke up.

"Gone to look at something."

"What?"

"You just go to sleep, Samuel." Harrison's voice was cross-sounding. "Just go to sleep and leave me be, you hear?"

But I didn't like being in that silent church room by myself, not with that iron spider hanging over my head and the baby buried in the floor. So I crept after Harrison. An oil lamp still flickered in Reverend Pry's small room. Harrison stood by the table, gathering up scraps of paper.

"You lookin for something, Harrison? Maybe I can find it," I said, sliding myself real easy into the room.

Harrison heaved a sigh. "Why you always after me, Samuel? Lordy, you don't ever leave me alone." He looked up and glared at me. "You want to know what I'm doin?"

I nodded.

"Well, you better keep yo' mouth shut," he said, shaking his finger at me. "And don't you say one word about it." He waved the scraps of paper in his hand. They had all the spiderweb words that Mr. Keepheart and Reverend Pry had been writing down. "I'm takin them. They ain't nothin but trouble."

"What?"

"Don't want no whitefolks reading 'bout me and you. I been thinkin. Say Mas'er Hackler or Miz Catherine reads it. Say one of them white patrollers reads it. They gonna be circling us like buzzards, sure enough."

None of this had crossed my mind.

"And know what my first master did 'fore he sold me years and years ago? I remember it plain as yesterday—" Harrison kept on. "He took out his fancy quill pen and wrote something down on a piece of paper. And Old Mas Hackler did the same when he bought me later on . . . know what I'm sayin, Samuel? I don't like writing atall, nothin good comes outta putting down words." Harrison snuffed out the lamp and took the papers back into the church room.

"You keepin them?" I asked.

"Course not," he snorted.

And he walked to a half-open window, tore the paper to pieces, and flung the writing out into the darkness. Stunned, I watched the scraps of paper flutter away. My whole story, the first story anyone had ever written down about me, was gone on the night wind.

Carryin On

I couldn't find a way to fall asleep that night. Even with the pile of blankets, the benches were hard as river rocks. And I didn't like sleeping in the big church room with all of the glass windows looking in on us. I thought about Master Hackler and Cassius searching for us somewhere in the darkness and putting up notices about us on trees and barns. Maybe they were circling closer and closer, creeping up to the church to catch us—

Heaving a sigh, I pulled all of the blankets onto the floor.

"That you, Samuel?" I heard Harrison mumble. "Settle down. Just git to sleep and settle down, child. I can't take no more of you."

Smoothing my tangle of blankets on the floor, I crawled under them and tried to keep my eyes from opening every half minute to check those dark windows. But then my mind started thinking about the baby in Mr. Keepheart's story, and I fell into a terrible-real dream about somebody else being buried under the whitefolks' church floor.

The church was dark as pitch, but the Reverend and Mr. Keepheart were shaking me awake. "Get up, Samuel," they were saying, with strange looks on their faces. "Wake up, so we can get underneath the floor."

I kept on asking them what had gone wrong, but they just

shook their heads and began rolling up the striped carpet until they had cleared a space the size of a man. Then Reverend Pry and Mr. Keepheart began to cut a large square out of the church floor. Cutting through the wood, their saw blades made a sound so sharp and terrible, I had to cover my ears.

When the hole was finished, they lifted up the wood planks, set them away, and called me to look inside. Leaning over the edge, I saw nothing at first. And then I began to notice what looked like stars and wisps of clouds, and the moon—as if they had cut a hole that opened not to the earth, but to the night sky.

"Move away, Samuel," the Reverend said quietly. "We need to place this poor soul inside."

I looked up to see them holding what seemed to be a large person, wrapped in a gray blanket. Mr. Keepheart held the place where the head seemed to be, and the Reverend held the feet. Their backs bent under the weight.

"Has someone died?" I asked, a terrible fear rising.

The Reverend gave me a sad look. Mr. Keepheart looked away.

"Who's that who died?" I said louder. "Tell me who's died."

"Your friend, the old man," the Reverend said softly. "I'm so sorry . . ."

And then they lowered the gray bundle into the dark hole and let it go. The bundle floated away, getting smaller and smaller, spinning and turning, as they held on to me, and I screamed and cried for Harrison.

- - -

"Why you lyin on that floor, hollerin like the Devil got hold of you?" Harrison's hand wrapped around my arm, and he gave me a hard shake. "Stop your carryin on, Samuel! Nothin's gonna hurt you. You just dreaming. Wake up now." Harrison shook me again. "Wake up!"

My heart pounded, and my eyelids felt heavy as two bricks trying to open.

"We still in the church?" I whispered.

Harrison gave a long sigh. "Far as I know. But I ain't sleepin none. That's fo' sure."

I opened my eyes to see him giving me a mean stare that said I was being more trouble than I was worth again.

I tried to remember what Lilly always said about bad dreams. Was it bad luck to tell them out loud, or bad luck to keep them quiet?

"Everything looked real as life," I told Harrison.

He shook his head tiredly. "Huh, sho' it did."

"I saw them cut a hole in the floor and bury somebody below the church, same as they did to that baby Mr. Keepheart tol' us about. They cut a big hole in the floor and set a person inside, and I tried to stop them. I hollered and kicked and screamed, and they wouldn't pay no attention . . ."

Only thing I didn't say was that the person they had been burying was Harrison.

Harrison pressed his lips into one tight line. "You need to grow up from believing in bad dreams, if you ask me. You is old enough now, Samuel, to grow up a little." He leaned back against the church bench and closed his eyes. "Shoulda known that story would make its way into your head. Shoulda known."

I felt ashamed for the way my mind was always making up things. Seemed like it sprouted weeds worse than a garden.

" 'Nough that," Harrison said, rubbing his eyes. "No more dreamin, you hear? We need to be getting some sleep now." He stood up and shuffled back to his own bench. "You better not wake me again," he called out in the darkness.

I put Mr. Keepheart's piece of barley candy in my mouth, and I didn't dream, or even stir from the floor, until a hand rocked me awake in the morning. The strange thing was, the hand that shook my shoulder was brown-skinned and a woman's.

Ham, Eggs, and Miz Kettle

"Wake up, child. Time's a-wasting," a voice said.

At first, I thought it was Lilly's voice, thought she was getting me up to milk the cows or split kindling or carry out the ash bucket. But a big colored woman with a red headwrap stared down at me, hands on her hips.

"Mornin," the woman said, leaning closer, and I saw how her eyes didn't look in the same place. One eye seemed to be looking at my face and the other, at the top of my head. "They tol' me you is called Samuel. That your name?"

"Yes," I said quiet.

"What'd you say? I didn't hear nothin but air talkin."

"YES," I said louder.

"Huh, that's better." The cross-eyed woman nodded and folded her big arms. "I got a name, too, but you don't call me that, you just call me Miz Kettle. MIZ KETTLE. That's my made-up name," she repeated. "And my husband, he got a name too, but you call him Ham, and my dog, he called Eggs."

None of this made any sense to me. Where had Reverend Pry and Mr. Keepheart gone to? Who was the cross-eyed woman? Why did she call herself Miz Kettle? And why was she hiding in the church with me and Harrison?

Harrison.

My heart thumped as I sat up and looked over at the white

bench where Harrison had been sleeping. Even in the gray morning light, I could see that the bench was empty.

A terrible fear seized me. I turned and stared at the other benches. All empty. The striped carpet stretched into the shadows like straight paths leading away.

Reverend Pry and Mr. Keepheart had buried Harrison below the church.

"Where's Harrison?" I said, my voice rising. "He was sleepin on that bench. Where'd he go to?" I jumped up and called out his name.

"Harrison!" It echoed loud in the empty church.

Miz Kettle grabbed hold of my arm. "Stop that, child," she said, one eye staring mean, the other looking off mean. "That old man ain't gone nowhere at all. Gone there." She waved her hand at the door to Reverend Pry's small room. "He'll be coming back in one-half minute. You just sit here and be good 'til he does, you listenin to me?"

She let go of my arm then and started picking up my blankets.

"Where's Mr. Keepheart?" I asked.

"Don't know no Mr. Keepheart," Miz Kettle said, holding a blanket under her round chin and bringing in the corners to fold it.

"Reverend Pry?"

She pressed her lips together. "No."

"The Widow Taylor bring you here?"

Miz Kettle's big shoulders heaved up and down. "Me and Ham and Eggs don't know NOBODY," she said, giving me a hard look. "That's the way it is. We just the movers who take you from here to there. Nobody knows us and we don't know nobody, see?"

Then the door of the Reverend's room opened, and out came Harrison looking like someone else. My mouth fell open.

All Harrison's white hair, even his ragged beard, had turned black. A low-crowned straw hat rested on his head. He wore overall pants and a worn, checked shirt I'd never seen before.

"Look like a fool in sheep's clothing," he snorted. "Boot grease on my beard. Hat like whitefolks'. I ain't goin nowhere in these clothes you give me."

That made Miz Kettle mad. I could see her big shoulders go up like bread dough rising, and her face pinch together. "Me and Ham's the boss of here." She put her hands on her hips and stared at Harrison. "And we does the leading and you does the following. You don't follow us, you get handed over to them crackers who's after you, you hear what I'm sayin, old man?"

Harrison sat down on one of the white benches then and fixed his eyes on the wall. He didn't say a word, only pressed his lips together and shook his head back and forth.

"Go on," Miz Kettle said, giving me a push. "Go on. Get ready, Samuel. There's clothes in that little room for you. We already be late enough. Don't want no more trouble."

But when I got to the room, all I found was a faded sunbonnet and a cotton striped dress lying across the back of a chair. I went out in the church to tell Miz Kettle, and she stopped and looked at me like I had lost my last crumb of sense.

"You think you just gonna walk around out there"—she waved her hand at the windows—"looking the same as you does now? You think your ol' master is gonna let you slip by him wearing the same old clothes he give you?" She pointed her finger at the Reverend's room. "You go on in there and put on that dress and be purely glad you got me and Ham helping you run off."

Sitting in one of the Reverend's chairs, I stared at that cotton striped dress. It had stitch patches and yellow fire burns all along the bottom edge, so I knew a girl had worn it, one time or another. All of Lilly's dresses were burned from catching sparks.

Last thing I wanted to do was wear some girl's dress.

"You comin, Samuel?" Miz Kettle called from the church, sounding mad.

I picked up the dress and shook it hard, as if it was crawling full of bedbugs. Then I peeled off my rain-stiff clothes and slid the dress over my head, quick as anything. I took my momma's gray yarn from my trousers and tied the yarn around my neck to keep it safe. Then I pulled on that sunbonnet. But I couldn't see anything except one small circle the size of a dinner plate in front of me. Almost walked into the doorjamb.

"There now," Miz Kettle said when I came into the church room. "Ain't that some kind of dis-guise. Can't even see his boy's face."

"Lord, have mercy," I heard Harrison whisper.

"All right, we's ready." Miz Kettle smacked her brown hands together.

"We ain't goin out in daylight looking like this." Harrison's voice was loud. I turned my head to see him. "No, we ain't. Me and Samuel is stayin here 'til it's night and dark." He leaned back against the church bench and folded his arms across his chest.

Miz Kettle walked over real slow. She was a big kind of woman. "Then you and the boy's gonna get caught by the night patrols," she said, staring down at Harrison with her cross-eyes. "They gonna see two black fools sneakin down the road late at night and know you run off. Only things that go sneaking round Ripley, O-hio, at night is horse thieves and runaways." Her chest heaved in and out, in and out, breathing hard.

"Me and Samuel's gonna take a wagon," Harrison said. "And hide inside it."

"Don't see no wagon," Miz Kettle said, looking around. "You see a wagon somewheres?"

Harrison was quiet for a long while. Like he was thinking hard. Then he heaved a loud sigh and stood up. "Go on" was all he said, waving his arm, angry. "Go on."

"Lord-ee." Miz Kettle pushed in front of us, her dress swaying back and forth like a blanket on a clothesline. "Follow me."

We went out of the church the same way we came in, through the Reverend's room. Outside, it was foggy and gray-looking. No morning sun at all. The yard was empty, only thing left was the mud tracks where all the wagons and carriages had been.

Miz Kettle stood half-in and half-out of the door, talking to us. "You walk on past the church and down that church road, 'til you sees a wood-plank bridge." She pointed. "In front of that bridge is an ol' tree stump, big as a tabletop. You set by that tree stump and wait till Ham and Eggs comes by and gets you." One eye looked hard at me and the other at Harrison. "You understand what you s'posed to do?" It gave me a strange feeling, as if there were two people inside her head.

"Yes'm." Harrison said sharply. "We does."

And then he hobbled away without another word. When we got farther down the road, Harrison turned and looked back at the church. The door was closed and Miz Kettle was gone.

"You keep yo' head down so they don't see inside that bonnet, Samuel," he whispered. "And you let me talk if there's talkin. And if there's trouble, you take to your heels and run like lightning into the woods. You don't wait for me, or nobody else." He spit at the ground. "I don't like this disguisin and walkin in daylight atall. Not atall. Anyone with eyes can see I ain't young and you ain't a girl."

The man that Miz Kettle had called Ham was already waiting by the tree stump when we got there. He was a skinny black fellow, leaning back on his elbows and smoking a yellow clay pipe. A longhaired dog was following his nose in circles around the bottom of the stump.

"Mornin. I'm Ham," the fellow said in a way that didn't sound friendly or not. The dog sidled over, but he wouldn't give my hand a lick, just sniffed at me and Harrison.

The fellow looked up at the gray sky and puffed lazily on his pipe.

"Good day for fishin," he said.

"Lady told us you was s'posed to take us somewhere." Harrison's voice was cross. "You just gonna sit there smokin your pipe and talking 'bout fishin, or you gonna take me and Samuel where you is s'posed to be taking us?"

"Well, now, I don't know," the fellow said slowly. Reaching behind him, he pulled up a whole stringer of fish from the tall grass, as if they'd just been swimming there. "Said it's a good day for fishin, didn't I?"

I stared at the fat, yellow-bellied fish, my mouth wide open.

The man squinted at Harrison. "Old Man Know-All died last year, I think. 'Less you be him."

Chuckling to himself, Ham slid off the stump. The dog jumped and snapped at the dripping tails of the fish. "Like I says before, it's a mighty good day for fishin, ain't it? You want to carry this string of fish we caught this morning?" he said to Harrison. "Or not?"

Harrison just took the stringer of fish. Didn't say a word.

"All right, then. The *girl* you be calling *Samuel*"—he gave Harrison a crooked grin—"she gonna carry your fishing poles."

Ham handed two fishing poles to me. "And you and her gonna just walk up this road, real slow and easy, like you been fishin in the creek real early, see? Me and Eggs, we walk ahead and keep a lookout. Be a few miles of walking maybe, but when I turn off the road, that's where we stop and meet again."

Ham whistled for his dog and started down the road.

"Lord, have mercy," I heard Harrison say under his breath. "Come on, Samuel."

But it gave me a jumpy feeling to sneak along a road in daylight pretending to be someone else. I couldn't see a thing, and I kept pitching forward and tripping on account of that sorry old dress dragging in the dirt.

"You the worst girl I ever seen," Harrison said over his shoulder. "Pick up yo' feet."

The only good thing was that no one came riding down the road.

And then someone did.

A Stringer of Fish

Voices and a jangle of wagon chains started up far behind us. We were walking a steep part of the road. "Something's comin," I said to Harrison.

"Keep walkin," he answered without turning around. "Just keep walkin and keep yo' head down."

Ham was so far ahead, all you could see was a smudge of brown that was his coat and a smudge of fur that was the dog, Eggs. He didn't care a straw about us, seemed like. Wasn't watching at all.

The wagon pulled closer. I could tell it was a wagon instead of a carriage by the creaking sound of the wheels. Sounded like big tree limbs swaying in the wind. Master Hackler had an old carry-all wagon, my mind said. What if Master Hackler was coming up the hill toward us?

Keep walkin, keep walkin, keep walkin.

A voice cursed at the horses to pull harder. I strained my ears to hear the names of those horses. I thought I heard Nap and Red, and when I heard those names, I let out some of the breath I was holding. Master Hackler's workhorses were called Web and Hall. But if it wasn't Master Hackler, it could be just about anybody, maybe white patrollers following us and chasing us down.

Keep walkin. Keep walkin. Keep walkin.

I kept my head down and tried not to catch my feet on the edge of that old dress. What was it the river man had said?

Walk as if you have the perfect right to do so, keep your shoulders back, swing your arms. Don't scuttle around like a bent-over black beetle, or they'll know that's exactly what you are—

A team of grays rattled past, pulling a wagon piled high with barrels and stove wood. I saw the wagon pass Harrison, who was walking in front of me. Then the creaking and rattling slowed.

"Whoa, boys," the wagoner said, and the horses came to a halt in the middle of the road. There was silence first, like the wagoner was looking us over, and then he called to me and Harrison. "You, darkies, come on over here."

My feet stopped. Felt like they had turned to lead.

The wagoner leaned over the side of the wagon. I could see his wide back with a dark stain of sweat from shoulder to shoulder. He pointed to Harrison. "Let me see what you got there in your hands," he said. "Hold up them fish, so I can get a good look at them, boy."

Harrison stepped closer to the wagon and lifted the string of fish. I could see the fish dangling and turning in the air. Me and Harrison were just like those fish, I thought, dangling in the air, barely breathing.

"You and the girl catch all them pretty fish this morning?" The man's voice was sharp and mean as a fishhook.

"Yes," Harrison said real low.

I ducked my head down and kept my eyes on the ground. Looked at the ruts and the horseshoe prints and the broken-up rocks and the dung piles. Didn't want him to see there wasn't any girl inside that bonnet.

"Ain't that nice," the wagoner said. "But I think you should give a few of them fine-looking fish to me, don't you?" Looking up quick, I saw the fellow reach down and tug the string of fish out of Harrison's hand. "Whitefolks got to eat supper too," he said.

After the man took the fish, Harrison didn't move. He just stood next to that wagon with his arms stiff at his sides. Looked like he turned into a block of wood.

"Tell you what." The man twisted the string of fish this-away and that-away, looking at them. "Since you been good enough to fish for me this morning, it wouldn't be right if I didn't leave something for you." And in a flash, the wagoner laid that string of fish on his wagon seat, thumped the head off the smallest one, and threw it at the ground in front of Harrison's feet. "There you go, darkie. Now you and that girl of yours got some fish to eat for your supper." He leaned his head back and laughed loud as the wagon pulled away.

Me and Harrison just stood on the side of the road after that, like we were nothing but a pair of old fence posts stuck in the dirt. "You remember me telling you how my ol' master's son caught me fishin one night when I was young?" Harrison said real quiet.

I nodded.

"They went and gave me a lash for every one of them fish I caught that night. You remember me telling you 'bout that? They said the pond wasn't mine, and the night wasn't mine, and the fish wasn't mine." Harrison looked down at the fish head lying in the road. It was nothing but a sad triangle with one staring eye.

"Got eleven scars on my back from them fish, Samuel, and the whole time my master was laying his cowhide across my back, know what I was thinkin?" Harrison looked at me. "I was thinkin that someday when I got myself free, I was gonna have me my own pond in the north, and I was gonna own every one of them fish in my pond, right down to the muddy bottom."

He picked up the fish head. "Walked all this way north to find out it ain't no different here atall. Nothing belongs to us here neither. Whitefolks own all the ponds, all the fish, and they gonna take whatever belongs to us, down to the very bottom. Don't matter where we go, Samuel. You and me and all the colored people in this world ain't worth—"

He flung the fish head hard into the woods. "Nothing."

Up ahead, Eggs started barking. Ham stood at the top of the hill, waving his arms. Waving and waving at us to keep walking.

"We s'posed to keep movin?" I asked.

"Go on." Harrison gave me a hard push. "You go on up the hill and when you catch up to that skinny fellow, you tell him that I ain't walkin all the way to Canaday," he snapped. "Don't even want to go to Canaday no more. No, I doesn't."

Green Murdock

Ham didn't listen to me or Harrison, though.

When Harrison got to where Ham was waiting, he tried to tell him that we weren't going any farther. "You can just leave us right here," Harrison said. "A wagon or a horse or the Lord himself can come and git us. I ain't walkin no more today."

But Ham just puffed slow on his pipe, and said it was only a stone's throw farther to the house of a man named Green Murdock, and that was the only place he was supposed to leave us. Green Murdock would take us somewhere after that.

"Where's he gonna take us to?" Harrison asked.

"Don't know," Ham said.

"How far we got to go 'til we see Canaday?"

"Don't know."

"Where we at now?"

"Don't know." Ham shrugged his shoulders, and whistled for Eggs. "I only take you from here to there. This morning, you was there and now you is here."

"Lord Almighty." Harrison rolled his eyes.

Ham kept on walking, down a small path through a woods of ash and oak trees. "One thing 'bout Green Murdock, though," Ham said over his shoulder. "Say he's a white fellow. That gonna worry you? 'Cause he ain't nothin but a peddler. Just an ol' white peddler fellow."

"A peddler?" Harrison said sharply, and I knew exactly what he was thinking.

Lilly used to say all peddlers were nothing but liars and cheats. "They talk outta the sides of their mouths, every single one of them," she would tell me when they came to the kitchen door. They were always trying to sell something to Miz Catherine, who was fond of buying fancy things, and Lilly would get a tongue-lashing every time they came. She'd get in trouble from Master Hackler if she let them in, and from Miz Catherine if she didn't.

Harrison went right up next to Ham, making his steps match Ham's long ones. "I hear you right? You sayin me and Samuel got to throw our luck on some no-good white peddler?"

"There's his house," Ham nodded, blowing little puffs of smoke.

At the end of the footpath stood a poor-looking plank house. Its small front porch sagged into the ground, and orange trumpet vines grew all over it like they were trying to push right in. In the field behind the house, there was a tumbledown barn and a sagging old woodshed.

"Looks like Green Murdock's wagon ain't come back yet," Ham said. He put his hands in his pockets and stood in the middle of the yard, like he didn't know what to do. "Guess you just gonna have to hide yourselves in his woodshed 'til it does."

Walking across the yard, he pushed open the crooked

woodshed door. "Nothin fancy," he said, setting a stick against the door to hold it open and looking inside real quick. "But he ain't gonna be gone long. Just out sellin things prob'ly." He waved his hand at the damp-smelling darkness. "Go on in."

Me and Harrison stepped inside.

Ham stuck his head through the open door. "Don't you worry. Green Murdock's gonna be back here in no time—" And without another word, he pushed the door shut and left me and Harrison in the middle of the darkness.

It was a long time before someone came.

We sat there in the closed-up woodshed, listening to the birds call outside, and a big yellow hornet buzz and peck at the window. Truth is, the sound of those birds made me feel worse inside. I thought about all those birds soaring around the treetops while we were hunched over like rats in the woodshed. My stomach grumbled. Last thing we had eaten was the loaf of bread at the whitefolks' church. Running and hiding. Seemed like that's all we had done for days and days. How many days had it been? I tried to count. Was it five or six since we had run off? There's nowhere in this whole United States that a runaway is safe, the river man had said. Would me and Harrison be running and hiding our whole lives?

"Hear something coming," Harrison said, tapping my arm.

There was the sound of a wagon rattling into the yard. I pushed back the girl's bonnet so I could keep an eye out. I didn't think anybody would know that we were hiding in the wood-shed, but I guess they did. The woodshed door creaked open not a half-minute later.

"Well, dog bite my tail," a voice boomed. "What fine colored folks have I got hiding in my shed today?"

I could see a short white fellow standing in the doorway. He had a shiny circle of bald skin on the top of his head, and by the looks of his clothes, he was fond of food.

"Come out in the light and show yourselves," the too-loud voice kept on. "Unless you are thinking about sitting in my wet and miry woodshed all day."

"You just stay quiet behind me," Harrison whispered over his shoulder.

Keeping my eyes on the edge of that dress so I wouldn't trip and fall over, I stepped outside the woodshed behind Harrison. But once I got there, a strange and peculiar feeling came over me. I felt the warm afternoon air on my face, and I saw light, plain as day, all around me. Reaching for where that girl's bonnet should have been, I felt nothing sitting on the top of my head.

Harrison shot me a look. "Samuel," he hissed. "Git that bonnet on."

But the white fellow put his hand over his eyes and laughed loud enough to send spit flying all over as he gasped and chuckled. Never saw any whitefolks ever laugh that way before.

"Don't you worry 'bout that bonnet," he said, trying to take in breaths of air. "That ain't nothing. I've seen colored girls dressed as boys, boys dressed as girls, women in their husbands' clothes, and men pretending to be poor widows."

Chuckling, he held a finger to his lips. "You don't need to breathe a single word about who you are or what master you ran off from. That's what I always tell the colored folks that come here. I tell them that Green Murdock holds secrets about as well as an upside-down cup holds water."

He started toward the house. "I'll just call you Young and Old, if that's fine with you. Or—" He stopped and pointed at me. "Now, this would be downright humorous. I'll call you Old and him"—he pointed to Harrison—"Young."

Even Harrison cracked a little smile at that.

"So, Old and Young, are you as hungry as a shilling, a half-dollar, or a whole dollar?" he said. " 'Cause I have everything from a half-chewed piece of corn cake—which'll cost you nothing—to a fine smoked ham in my wagon, depending on what you have the money to pay for eating." He squinted at us. "Paper money or coins are all the same to me. Which one might you be carrying, Old and Young?"

Harrison didn't answer, and Green Murdock got a down look on his face.

"Don't tell me that you ran off from your master without a shred of money," he said. "Me and my poor horse have to eat, don't we? And keep a roof over our heads? Only way I make a living is by peddling things." He shook his head. "All of this helping folks is just about putting old Green Murdock in the poorhouse these days."

I remembered the five coins we had given to the widow lady and how we still had a few left over. Why was Harrison not breathing a word about them?

"We got a little something, maybe," Harrison said uneasy-like. "Enough money to eat, I s'pose."

"Enough money to eat?! Well, dog bite my tail, Young—" Green Murdock broke into a grin and slapped his leg. "I'm just a poor peddler and even I don't eat MONEY!"

I could see Harrison's shoulders go up fast, like he didn't think Green Murdock was being funny at all. Reaching into his pocket, Harrison pulled out the leather pouch of coins. "Here," he said sharply, holding out two coins. "This be 'nough for me and Samuel's supper?"

Green Murdock took both coins and slipped them into his boots. "Didn't mean to say that about running off without a shred of money, Young." He patted Harrison's shoulder. "I'm the kind that always helps folks and does what I can. Any soul around here would tell you that about old Green Murdock.

"Now, let's see if I can find you that good smoked ham I told you about. It came all the way from Cin-cin-nati. Almost walked out of town by itself. You go on in the house"—he pointed—"while I have a look around my wagon."

Green Murdock paused and grinned at me. "Maybe I'll even bring a new tow-linen shirt and trousers for the boy."

Only thing was, he couldn't find the fancy ham. He came back carrying a small slab of bacon and a bag of potatoes instead. "Don't you worry," he told us, throwing kindling onto the fire until the flames licked halfway up the chimney. "I can cook this piece of bacon good enough that it'll taste just like that fancy ham."

Truth is, the tow shirt and trousers weren't new either. When I put them on, I saw the trousers had little chew holes from mice, and the shirt was splattered with mud. But I was purely glad to be free of that girl's dress, so I didn't breathe a word.

Green Murdock told us to have a look around while he was cooking. "Go on. Look at all the things I sell," he said, waving his arm around the room. "Just don't touch anything. That's what I always tell the colored folks. Can't have all my china broken and my fine embroideries ruined."

Right away, my eyes fell on a plain pine box leaning up against a wall. Size of a person. Green Murdock chuckled, seeing me staring at that coffin. "I sell everything folks need from birth to death, and anything else that happens to someone in between."

He lifted a china bowl from an open crate full of straw. "These fancy willowware bowls came all the way from England. Aren't they something to see?" He held the bowl in front of me and Harrison, turning it this way and that. "Sold two of them this morning to old Rose Waverly in Red Oak.

"She's cheap as a secondhand toothbrush," he said, grinning. "But when I stopped at her house this morning, I just happened to notice a broken bowl swept off to the side of her porch. And a little idea came into this clever head of mine." Green Murdock tapped his forehead.

"I told Rose Waverly I had just the thing to fix her broken bowl. Old Green Murdock can make it look as good as new, I told her. And while she was fixing me a piece of pie, I brought out two of my best willowware bowls and set them near the porch. Then I called her outside and said, 'Why, DOG BITE MY TAIL, your broken bowl has changed into two fine, new bowls, Miz Waverly!' "

Green Murdock shook his head. "Well, you shoulda seen the look on her face. She bought those bowls from me right then and there." He walked over to the hearth and turned the side of bacon. "Dog bite my tail," he said, licking the grease off his cooking fork. "Sometimes I think I'm the best peddler on this side of the Ohio."

"Sure enough," Harrison answered, rolling his eyes at me.

I thought about how we had given Green Murdock two silver coins for nothing more than a side of bacon, a bag of mealy potatoes, and half-worn clothes. Maybe we weren't much smarter than old Rose Waverly.

After supper, Green Murdock brought out a deck of cards

and told us he would foretell our future. His white hands slid the deck of cards toward Harrison.

Lilly always said cards were nothing but trouble. When Seth dragged me into playing a game with him, she would always pinch my arm and whisper, "You let him win, Samuel. You just be as awful slow and addle-headed as you have to be, but you let him win. We don't want no hard times."

Harrison pushed the cards back. "Me and Samuel don't want none of our future read," he said.

But Green Murdock leaned back in his chair and waved his hands. "Go on. Go on. Go on. Make sure they ain't anything but plain old ordinary playing cards. I'll even let you shuffle them, if you want to, Young. Make it even harder for me."

When Harrison didn't pick up the cards, Green Murdock crossed his arms, frowned a little, and said, "Dog bite my tail, Young, you want me to shuffle the cards too?"

Harrison didn't answer.

"All right, I will, I will." Green Murdock shook his head slowly back and forth.

Me and Harrison didn't have a choice in the matter. Seemed like he was going to foretell our future, whether we wanted to know it or not. Shuffling the cards with his thumbs, he put four cards facedown on the table.

Then he looked across the table at me. "Now, Old, you turn the first card faceup on the table. Go on"—he tapped the first card with his finger—"turn this one over."

I shot a quick look at Harrison, who was staring straight ahead, not paying any mind, and I turned over the first card.

Green Murdock nodded and smiled. "You can turn over the others now too."

I set the cards faceup on the table—a ten of diamonds, an ace of clubs, a five of spades, and an ace of spades.

Green Murdock leaned forward, staring at the cards. He drummed his fingers on the table. "Well, now," he said, frowning, "I see a few unlucky cards here. You had any bad luck up 'til now, Old?"

"Why?" I said, looking closer at the cards, as if our bad luck was drawn right on those squares. As if maybe there would be a picture of Master Hackler or Cassius. Or bloodhounds hunting for us.

"Well," Green Murdock said, tapping the first card, "the ten of diamonds ain't all bad. It just means to look out for a long journey."

Harrison snorted. "We already on a long journey. Don't take no one smart to tell us that."

Green Murdock smacked his hands together. "Dog bite my tail, see there. That fortune has already come true. Green Murdock and his cards are always right . . ." He leaned back in his chair and clucked like an old red hen.

Harrison squinted his eyes and tapped the next card with his finger. "How 'bout that one?"

"Hmmm . . ." Green Murdock rolled his eyes toward the

ceiling. "The ace of clubs means, let's see . . . I think it means an important, ah, letter or SIGN, that's right, a sign is coming from somewhere. Have you gotten any signs?" He glanced around the room, as if he was expecting them to come sailing through the ceiling.

"What kinda sign?" Harrison said sharp, fixing his eyes on Green Murdock like he knew something that Green Murdock didn't.

"Ah, hmmm, well," Green Murdock stuttered. "A small sign, a very small sign, from somewhere far away. Somewhere that people live. But a good, ah, sign, from what I can see, that is." He hurried on. "Now, the next card—the five of spades— that is one of those unlucky cards. It means something unexpected is coming."

"Ain't nothin sure in this life," Harrison said, tapping the card with his hand. " 'Cept death."

"Well, now, yes, that's the truth, Young." Green Murdock chuckled at Harrison and shook his head back and forth. "I'm just telling you to keep an eye out for little things you ain't been expecting. That's all."

And then, quick as anything, he slid the last card off the table and turned it facedown. "And we don't need to talk about the ACE of spades," he said, stacking the cards and putting them away in his coat. "Because you folks probably know that is the most unlucky card of all."

I started to say that I didn't have the smallest idea what the ace of spades meant, but Green Murdock pushed his chair back and stood up fast. "Dog bite my tail, I am worn out as an old shirt," he said, yawning. "All this card reading and future telling is hard work. Don't know why I do it day in and day out. Never get so much as one copper cent for all my work helping folks."

Harrison tapped the floor with his foot. "It gonna cost us money to sleep here?" he said. " 'Cause I ain't laying my head down if it is."

Green Murdock leaned his head back and laughed real loud again. "Course not." He grinned. "Won't cost you a thing, but you are awful humorous, Young. Awful humorous. Don't know when I have ever met an old colored fellow who talks smart like you."

He kept on chuckling to himself as he walked into his bed-chamber. "Good night," he hollered, and not a minute later, we heard him breathing and snoring in his bed. Me and Harrison were left to bank the ashes, scrape and wash the plates, and snuff out the candles.

"Don't like him atall," Harrison whispered as we fixed a pile of blankets for sleeping near the hearth. "He don't see things and read minds anymore than I does. Just goes and steals money away from folks." Harrison pulled a blanket around his shoulders. "Nothing but a liar and cheat. That's all he is. You and me gonna find someplace else tomorrow. I ain't stayin here one more day, Samuel."

But as I listened to the sound of Green Murdock snoring like an old pit saw in the darkness, I couldn't help thinking about that ace of spades again.

Why was it the most unlucky card of all?

When morning came, I knew.

Ace of Spades

Harrison woke up, burning with a fever.

"Don't know what come over me while I was sleepin," he moaned.

He threw off all of the blankets and then pulled them back on again, threw them off, and then pulled them back on again.

"Can't catch my breath. Seems like I got no air left to breathe," he whispered, pressing a trembling hand to his chest.

I felt weak all over, watching Harrison suffering and calling out.

Green Murdock was still half-asleep when I crept into his bedchamber to fetch him. "It ain't the yellow fever, is it?" he said, jumping up. He tugged on a pair of trousers and his broadcloth coat. "I knew something bad was coming when I saw that ace of spades last night. Dog bite my tail, I knew someone was gonna come down sick and die."

I could feel the snake wrap itself around my throat. Squeezing tighter and tighter until I couldn't speak at all.

Green Murdock leaned over a small table near the window. A whole field of bottles and tins sat on that table. Holding up one after another, Green Murdock took a swallow from a blue glass bottle and two small brown ones. "Doggone it," he said, wiping his hand across his mouth. "I don't want to catch the yellow fever from that old fellow with you, no, I don't. Nothing

scares me more than dying of something awful terrible like that."
The glass bottles rattled as he set them on the table and turned
back toward me.

"I can't keep you and him here any longer," he said, casting
his eyes down and buttoning his coat fast. "I have my rounds to
make, see, and my food is already getting low, feeding two extra
mouths, and now one of them is sick. And I can't be taking care
of all kinds of sick colored folks." He picked up a hat from the
floor and brushed off the dust. "Green Murdock's business is
peddling, not doctoring, see," he told me, turning the hat around
in his hands. "I don't know a thing about doctoring. I'm awful
sorry about that, see, but that's just the way it is."

He moved toward the bedchamber door. "I'll take you to
the Negro Hollow outside Hillsboro, how about that? There's
colored folks there. Those folks should take care of that old man
with you, don't you think?"

I could hear the sound of rain drumming on the roof, and
a low roll of thunder rumbled overhead. Green Murdock looked
up at the ceiling and frowned. "Storm's coming," he said, tugging
his hat down over his head. "Won't be long."

Holding a striped handkerchief to his face, he hurried
across the room where Harrison and me had been sleeping.
"Once I get my wagon loaded, you bring that fellow outside," he
said, opening the front door fast and waving his hand toward
Harrison. Then he shut the door and was gone.

After Green Murdock left the house, I wrapped all the

blankets I could find around Harrison's shoulders, one on top of the other like husks of corn, as if the thin, old blankets would somehow keep out trouble.

"We gotta move somewhere else," I told Harrison. "Green Murdock's takin us somewhere else."

"Where?" Harrison shivered as another tremble shook him.

"Place called Hillsboro."

"Don't know Hillsboro. Just let me lay here a while." Harrison sighed and closed his eyes. "Ain't got the strength to go nowhere."

"We gotta do what Green Murdock says," I tried to tell him.

"Leave me be," he whispered. "Go on and leave me be."

It took me forever to pull him to standing.

"I'm feelin awful downright bad, Samuel," he said, trembling. His fingers curled around my shoulder. "Awful downright bad."

I swallowed hard and tried to keep back all the tears that were filling up my eyes. "Just a little ways more," I said.

Harrison nodded toward the door. "Go on, Samuel. Move on. 'Fore I fall over."

Outside, the rain was coming down in heavy, splattering drops. I just stood there on the crooked front porch, staring up at the black clouds racked overhead. Little bits of white ice came down from some of those clouds and jumped in the yard, looking like kernels of popping corn.

"Lord," Harrison whispered.

"THE WAGON'S READY," Green Murdock hollered and waved at us from the middle of the yard. But me and Harrison stayed where we were, eyeing all that rain and ice coming down.

Hunching his shoulders against the rain, Green Murdock ran toward us. "You coming?" he yelled, standing at the foot of the porch steps, with water pouring off the sides of his hat. "My horse is already jumpy as spit. And the road to Hillsboro is gonna be a sea of mud if we don't start going."

Me and Harrison were soaked clear through by the time we got across that yard. When we reached the wagon, Green Murdock lowered the tailboard, and Harrison crawled into the wagon on his hands and knees. He leaned against a molasses barrel, eyes closed, water running in rivers down his face. I crawled in after him.

Green Murdock leaned his head inside the wagon. "Keep away from those good bolts of black silk in the corner," he said, pointing. "And be careful of the crates of crockery and glassware. And don't put your hands on anything that might break." Then he closed the canvas flaps and tied them down.

Me and Harrison were the only things in that wagon he didn't care about. That's what went through my mind. Black silk, glass, willowware bowls, he said. But not a word about me and Harrison.

"Gid-up," Green Murdock hollered to his horse.

Creaking and swaying, the wagon started down the road. A

row of wooden buckets tumbled over in the corner of the wagon bed, and everything rattled as the wheels rolled into one rut after another. Rain splattered on the canvas top, and outside, I could hear Green Murdock cursing at his horse.

Harrison moaned and tugged at the rain-soaked blankets around his shoulders. "We movin?" he whispered.

"Yes."

"You see anything for me to drink?" Harrison cast his feverish eyes around the dark wagon. "I am 'bout festered with thirst. You see anything to drink?"

Only thing I found was an old tin ladle. Holding it under the canvas, I tried to catch some of the rain coming off the canvas sides. But the rain ran every which-way in thin little rivers. Couldn't catch more than a trickle for Harrison.

"Better than nothin," he said, letting the little bit of cold rainwater run between his lips. "Better than nothin." After it was gone, he leaned back against the molasses barrel and closed his eyes. "I got something on my mind to tell you, Samuel," he whispered.

"What?" I said, looking over.

"You still got that roll of yarn? The one I brung along in the tow sack?"

I had almost forgotten the roll of yarn tied around my neck. The only thing the river man had let us keep. Slipping it over my head, I held it out for Harrison, and thought about my momma again, thought about her holding that same roll of yarn, years and years ago.

"Know where that yarn come from?" Harrison said.

"My momma."

"Know when it got left?"

"When she was taken away to Washington, Kentucky?"

Harrison shook his head. "Naw." He coughed hard and tugged at the blankets around his shoulders. "You recollect that June day, 'bout three months ago, when one of Mas'er Hackler's cows ate poison weed in the field and died, and that big rainstorm came over at night and beat down the corn?"

In my mind, I could see Master Hackler's brown milk cow lying in the field, legs stuck out like a piece of furniture, dead. And I remembered how Lilly had hollered and flapped her apron at it, yelling at it to get up, get up, because she knew we were gonna get in trouble for that cow dying.

"Well, something else happened that day that me and Lilly never did tell you, 'cause we was mixed up about what to do." Harrison heaved a sigh. "It 'bout harrowed up our souls, worrying."

He pointed to the gray yarn in my hand. "That roll of yarn come from your momma that day."

I stared at Harrison.

I knew my momma had been gone since the day she left in Master Hackler's wagon. No one had ever seen her again—not

Harrison or Lilly or me. She had been taken away to the court-house in Washington, Kentucky, with her head down in her hands, and she had never come back. That was the truth.

"My momma's gone," I said, closing my fingers around the yarn. "You know that, same as me. You is making up things in yo' head on account of the fever, Harrison."

"I ain't making up a thing." Harrison coughed. "Just look inside that yarn. Go on, now." He waved his hand. "Look."

I unraveled the tangle of yarn, and when I got to the mid-dle, something fluttered into my lap. A torn scrap of paper. I could see two small words written in brown ink on that paper. One word, an empty space, then another word.

"Paper says Chat-ham, Canaday," Harrison said, leaning over to look at it. He put his finger on each word. "Chat-ham, Canaday. The colored blacksmith who can read tol' me what it said. That's where your momma, Hannah, is."

I stared at Harrison. "My momma give this to you?"

"No." Harrison leaned back and closed his eyes. "It was a sign between me and Lilly and your momma. The day they took her away, 'bout ten years ago now, me and Lilly tol' her—you ever get free, you find a way to send us and Samuel some sign so's we know. Just send us a little kinda sign, we said, nothin much, or Mas'er Hackler will figure something is up."

Harrison picked up the tangle of yarn from my hands. "Your momma said if she ever got herself free, she'd send us a roll of gray wool yarn. 'That yarn be my sign,' she told us, because all her hands did is weave and spin for the Old Mas Hackler and his wife, and gray was the color of their no-good, worthless heads."

Harrison shook his head. "Me and Lilly never figured on that sign coming someday. We figured your momma was long gone. Same as being laid out in our little Negro burying-ground. When folks is sold off, you don't never see or hear from them again. Same as bein dead."

Harrison leaned back against the molasses barrel. The wagon creaked and groaned on the rough road. "The same day the cow died and the storm blew over, I found the yarn setting on my milk stool in the barn, plain as day. Don't know who brung it or how it got to be there. But when I saw it and found the scrap of paper inside, I knew, sure as anything, it was the sign from your momma tellin us she was free."

I thought about Green Murdock foretelling our future. Watch for a letter or sign coming, wasn't that what he had said? A little shiver went through me.

Harrison closed his eyes. "Knowing your momma was free just about worried us to death, 'cause we didn't know what to do about you. I tol' Lilly I was gonna take you to Canaday my ownself. And she didn't like that atall." He shook his head. " 'You as old as the hills,' she told me. 'How you gonna get all the way to Canaday with Samuel?' But I just said my mind was made up."

Harrison pulled the blankets tighter around his shoulders. "Wasn't gonna breathe a word to you till we got to Canaday and found your momma. Wasn't gonna breathe a word—"

A bad tremble shook him. "But Lord Almighty, I got the fever terrible," he said, his teeth knocking together. "I been worryin that maybe the Lord is coming to take me this time. What's Samuel gonna do if I leave him without telling him that his momma is free? That's what I been thinkin." He fixed his eyes on me. "So if anything happens to me, you keep on runnin, Samuel, you keep on going to Canaday, you hear me?"

"You gonna get better," I said loudly. "Nothing's gonna happen to you."

"How you know that, Samuel?" Harrison snapped. "You the Lord?"

Closing his eyes, he leaned back against the barrel to rest, and my heart thundered inside me.

Outside, the wagon swayed and rattled through the rainstorm. Tinware and baskets fell over and rolled loose in the wagon bed. Buckets tumbled down. Seemed like everything I knew, and didn't know, was rolling around in my mind like tinware and baskets . . . *my momma being free in a place called Chatham, Canaday . . . Green Murdock's fortunes all coming true . . . Harrison being terrible-sick with the fever . . . Lilly not wanting me to leave atall . . .*

You ain't allowed to cry, Lilly whispered in my mind.

Negro Hollow

It was late, almost dark, before Green Murdock came around to the back of the wagon to fetch us. As he untied the canvas flaps, all I could see was one little stripe of yellow in the sky. Everything else was woods and darkness, soaked full of rain.

"Dog bite my tail, I thought I would never get us here. You still in one piece, Young and Old?" Green Murdock peered into the wagon. "The Negro Hollow is just down this road, maybe a quarter mile, and if you hurry, you can get there before it's too dark to see, I imagine."

But Harrison was worse. As he slowly climbed out of the wagon, he was taken by a bad spell, and he could only lean against the side, eyes closed, his hand clutching at the blanket around his chest. "Can't take in a breath of air," he whispered.

"You," Green Murdock said, pulling hard on my arm. "Run to the Hollow and get some of the colored folks there. Tell them to hurry back here, fast as they can. I ain't gonna stay here long with him." He looked up at the sky and shook his head. "I knew this was gonna happen. Too sick to get out of my wagon. I knew this was gonna happen.

"Go on, run now." He gave me a hard push, and I started down the dark road, my feet sloppy and unsteady in the mud and ruts. Didn't even know what I was running toward. Just ran.

The road got narrow and more narrow, until it was only

two wagon tracks through weeds. Seemed like even those tracks were about to leave my feet and fade into the fields.

Ain't nothing here, my mind kept saying. *There's no Negro Hollow. What if Green Murdock has taken the wagon and left you in the middle of a woods? White patrollers could be riding anywhere around. Never gonna find your way back now even if you try.*

But then I saw the lights. Looked just like a flicker in the darkness. As I got closer, I could see a patch of silvery-gray houses. Most were leaning, one-room cabins next to a few wood frame houses. No more than a dozen in all.

Feeling trembly as leaves, I crept toward one of the houses. It had a square porch along one side. I set one foot at a time on that porch, keeping an ear toward the door. I could smell the sour-sharp smell of cabbage cooking, and it sounded like colored peoples' voices inside. Made me think of Lilly making cabbage soup for our supper. I raised my hand to knock.

But instead, the door flew open in front of me.

I caught my breath and froze.

A colored woman the size of Miz Catherine, maybe larger, filled the whole doorway in front of me. Her skin was pure black, the blackest skin I had ever seen. Black as an iron kettle.

Holding a skillet in one hand, she stared down at me, eyes snapping. "I saw you from the window. Why you creepin round my house? You lookin to take something that don't belong to you?" She raised the skillet as if to bring it right down on my head. "You lookin to make mischief with all I own in this world? Answer me straight now, child."

My feet stayed stuck where they were, like they were nailed to the porch, and nothing but a small whisper came out of my mouth. "Green Murdock, he tol' me to come here. Harrison's got a bad fever. He said to come here."

The woman narrowed her eyes until they were just two mean slits. "Don't know Green Murdock and don't know why he tol' you to come here," she said sharply. "Git off my porch, and don't you come callin round here again. I don't take care of no poor colored folk."

The door slammed shut, and there was the sound of heavy footsteps walking away. The tears that I'd been holding back came spilling out faster than I could stop them. Whole rivers of tears.

Then I heard a window opening near me. There was the scraping sound of someone nearby pushing up a window frame, slow and careful-like. It whispered through my mind that maybe the woman was going to aim the skillet at my head. But instead, a voice called out into the darkness.

"You there. Child," the voice said real low. "Go three doors down. They take you there. Go round back. Knock twice and twice again. Twice, twice again. Don't you forget." Then the window scraped closed, and when I looked around, I couldn't see a soul anywhere.

A shiver went clear through me.

I wanted to leave the Negro Hollow right then and run back down the road to Harrison and Green Murdock. Didn't want to go creeping around the tumbledown houses anymore. But you don't come back to whitefolks with empty hands, I knew that. If they tell you to do something, you do it.

So I crept toward the third house in the Negro Hollow. It was a small, white-painted house set in a dirt yard like the others. Go around back, the voice had said, so I slipped around the side of the house, keeping close to a row of bushes. There was a flickering lamp in the back window. Enough light to see that the stone steps in the back were all empty and swept clean. A broom leaned against the side of the house as if it had just finished sweeping.

It made me jumpy to see how everything was neat as a new pin, like the people inside were just waiting for someone to come and pay them a visit.

A colored woman's voice was talking in the house. A man's voice answered now and again, only I couldn't tell what they were saying, except for a word or two. I put one foot on the stone steps.

On the other side of the door, I could hear the sound of dishes being clattered together. "You want some of this pie, August? You hear me?" the woman's voice called loudly. "It just got done now."

I drew in my breath and raised my hand to knock. Knocked light and soft as I could, twice and twice again.

The feet paused, and the woman's voice stopped.

"August. August . . ." I heard someone whisper. "The door." There was the sound of quick footsteps moving back and forth as if they were running across the floor. Then the light in the back window went out, turning everything into darkness.

I had been sent straight into trouble.

In front of me, the door latch rattled. I dug my fingers into my palms, waiting to be hollered at or sent away.

"Why you come knocking here?" a low voice said as the door creaked open.

The skin on my neck prickled. Past the door, I could see nothing but darkness. The smell of snuffed-out candles drifted out.

"Tell us," the man's voice said, louder this time. "Tell us why you knocked, or you won't be setting one foot inside this house."

I couldn't think of a word to say. Just like the candles, all my words were snuffed out and gone.

A woman's voice jumped from another part of the shadows. "It's a child, August. A colored boy. You don't need to go scaring the life out of a poor child."

A chair scraped behind the door. "Now, how am I s'posed to see some child standing on the steps if I'm setting behind the door, Belle?"

"Well, that's who it is. I can see him standing in the doorway, plain as day. You gonna bring him in, August, or just leave him standing in the dark?"

"I tol' him to come in," the man's voice kept on.

"No, you didn't."

I shifted from one foot to the other, thinking about running off.

"Yes'm, I did."

"No, you did not."

The man behind the door heaved a loud sigh, and before I could turn on my heels and run, he came through the doorway, took ahold of my arm and pulled me into the house.

"That child be standing right now in the middle of your kitchen, Belle," the man said, closing the door with a hard push. "And I sho' hope he's a colored child, otherwise"—he paused and chuckled—"we gonna have to peel and pickle him for our supper."

"August!" the woman said sharply.

The man kept on chuckling. "You gonna light your lamp, Belle, so I don't fall over and shoot him with this pistol I'm holding?"

My heart jumped.

A woman's dress rustled in the darkness. "Lord, I don't know why you talk that way and why you fool with that ol' gun, August. You gonna kill somebody yet."

A lamp flared in front of me, and I found myself being stared at by a colored man and woman dressed in whitefolks' clothes. The woman had on a fancy green checked dress and a small white bonnet over her hair. The man was wearing a good brown-cloth coat and trousers.

They were both tall and strong-looking. If they hadn't been wearing whitefolks' clothes, they would have looked just like the field hands that Master Hackler hired every year. Only, none of his field hands would ever be caught dead in those fancy clothes. He would work them until there were no bones left for fine clothes.

"How you?" The man leaned closer, giving me a squint look.

"You can't ask a child questions pointing a gun at him." The woman flapped one hand in the air. "Go on and put that gun away, August."

"See, child," the man said, turning the flintlock pistol in his hands. "She's worrying 'bout something as old as George Washington himself. Only thing I keep it for is making sure it's always colored folks giving the signal and no whitefolks sneaking around, trying to catch us—"

"August."

"Yes'm." Walking over, August stuck the nose of the pistol in a clay pot beside the door. "There," he said, straightening up. "Don't know why you all the time fretting about a gun that ain't hit a thing in years, Belle."

The woman called Belle shook her head. "You nothing but trouble."

The colored man grinned. "Uh-huh, that's me." He nodded his head in my direction. "You gonna get the boy something to eat? He sho' looks like he could use something on them skinny bones."

"I imagine so," she said.

I looked down at my feet, not knowing what to say about Harrison and going back to the wagon where he was waiting.

Belle stepped closer and gave me a curious look. "You think he run off all by his ownself? Or other folks coming behind him?"

August shrugged his shoulders. "All I know is I threw down that whole pipe of tobacco I was smoking when he knocked on the door," he said. "And I'm gonna find it before any more folks start pouring in."

As August walked away, I tried to say how I had run off from Master Hackler with Harrison, and how he had been taken sick with a fever and was waiting by Green Murdock's wagon on the road to the Negro Hollow, and how we needed to hurry down the road to get him. But nothing I said seemed to make a bit of sense to them.

"Speak up, child," Belle said. "Who's Harrison? Someone else out there?"

August's eyes shot a quick look at the closed door. "You saying there's two blackfolks hiding outside? Green Murdock and Harrison? Or they inside a peddler's wagon? Which one is it?" he asked. "They both sick with a fever?"

But I hadn't even opened my mouth to answer when the door smacked open, and Harrison himself stood there in the doorway, leaning on his walking stick with both hands.

"You all right, Samuel?" he said in a trembling, far-off kind of voice. "You was gone and you didn't come back. I tol' that peddler to just go on with his wagon and leave us be. And I came looking. Didn't know what else to do. Looked everywhere in the Hollow, trying to find you."

Harrison's fever-bright eyes turned to stare at the man and woman standing behind me. "My name's Harrison. Who you?" he said sharp.

"August Henry." The colored man stepped forward and reached out his hand toward Harrison. But Harrison didn't move or raise his hand, just stayed where he was, so the man's hand stayed stuck in the air until he put it back down.

"And I'm Belle." The woman nodded, smoothing her dress with the flats of her brown hands.

"Belle," Harrison said, and the shadow of a smile crossed over his face. "Belle," he repeated. Then his eyes slid closed, and his body seemed to fold up on itself. Before any of us could move, Harrison's walking stick clattered out of his hands and his body crumpled to the floor.

"Belle," he whispered, and lay still.

And truth is, I fell to the floor too because I thought Harrison, who had looked after me my whole life, was dead.

Red Stars in a White Sky

Harrison had the lung fever.

After they had carried Harrison to the upstairs chamber and covered him with blankets, Belle came back to the open door where I was still holding Harrison's walking stick and staring out into the darkness, as if I had turned to a piece of stone.

"He run away with you?" she asked quiet.

"Yes,'m" I said, not turning around.

"You run from Kentucky?"

"Yes'm."

Belle said they had seen the lung fever before in other runaways that had come through. She said it was from being out in the damp woods and night chills too long.

I remembered sitting in that old tree in the downpour when Master Hackler had been looking for us, and sleeping in the woods when I had gotten us lost, and making Harrison pull himself out of that shallow river when I was feeling mad. "We don't die but once," he had said, driving his walking stick into the ground.

"Nothing you coulda done or not done," Belle said as if she could see all the thoughts in my mind, plain as day. "Some come down with the lung fever and some don't."

I looked at my hands curled around the top of the walking stick, and thought about Harrison's hands. "He gonna get well?"

"Well, now," Belle said real quiet. "Some does, yes, but

your friend's got the fever awful bad. Worse than we've seen in a long while. And me and August, we seen a lot."

I knew by the way her voice trailed away, and she cast her eyes down, that she meant Harrison's fever was bad, bad, bad. That I shouldn't be expecting anything good to happen. But somewhere inside me, I did. I know I did because my eyes were as dry as salt, dry as bones.

You don't cry unless someone is dying or dead.

Belle wiped her hands on her apron and told me she was going to mix up some brandy and egg for Harrison. "Why don't you close that door, and come help me, Samuel?" she said, trying to make her voice nice and pleasant. "That is your name, right? Samuel? No use standing there"—she reached over and pushed the door closed—"looking out into the darkness like that. You ever hear of brandy and egg for fevers where you come from?" Belle moved toward the kitchen table.

"No'm," I said, thinking about Lilly's fence-grass tea. That's what she always made for fevers. She would put fence-grass and water to boil over the fire, and she would stand there, stirring and tasting, until her whole cabin smelled sharp and green as the outdoors after a hard rain.

"Brandy and egg's my momma's old remedy. She was a slave in Mary-land, and one day, her master just set her free." Belle reached into a basket of eggs on the table, pulled out two, and cracked them on the side of the bowl. "He said, 'Eliza, you free,' just like that."

The yolks slid into the bowl, and Belle poured in brandy from a stoneware jug. "I was born a free person, and my brothers and sisters all free too. Imagine that. We just about the luckiest folks in the world, I suppose."

Seemed strange to hear a colored person saying they were free. I had never heard of any blackfolks who called themselves free before. Not on Master Hackler's farm. Only person who was almost free, I figured, was the colored blacksmith who could come and go from farm to farm, and who was allowed to read.

Belle stirred the bowl fast, sending yolk and brandy flying. "My momma, she's still living in Philadelphia, where she went after they set her free. She's 'bout the same years old as the man with you.

"There." Belle lifted the spoon to her lips and took a taste. "I put all my faith in her doctoring. If the brandy and egg don't do what it's supposed to, then the Lord has other plans, that's what she would say. You can't fool the Lord."

But that's exactly what we tried to do.

Me and Belle, and sometimes August, sat beside Harrison, spooning brandy and egg into his mouth, and pressing cold cloths on his skin, hour after hour. "Another little while or so, we gonna get his fever starting down," Belle would say, giving August a look. "Don't you worry, Samuel."

But Harrison's brown skin stayed hot and dry as sunbaked field dirt, and the water trailed off him, fast as we put it on.

"Tell me about Harrison and the place you run away from," Belle would say. She would try to cover up the uneven and trembling sound of Harrison's breathing with question after question. "Was Harrison the one who raised you? From the time you was a baby? What work did he do on your master's farm? How many slaves did your master keep? What did your master grow in his fields? Corn? Tobacco? Is the corn as tall here in Ohio as it was in Kentucky?"

Mostly, I only answered "yes'm" or "no'm," and kept my eyes on the quilt that covered up Harrison. The quilt had red stars in a white sky. "You like how fine and bright them stars look?" Belle would say as she smoothed her hand on the top of the quilt. "I cut and pieced those stars my ownself. Took forever."

On every one of the stars, I wished things. Foolish things. I would look at the center of those stars until I could see nothing but color in front of my eyes, like staring straight into the afternoon sun, and then I would make my wish.

I wished to be back at Master Hackler's farm, living just the same as always with Harrison and Lilly. I wished for Harrison to open his eyes and holler, "Let's get a-movin, Samuel." I wished for Lilly to run away and find us in the Negro Hollow.

When I was quiet for too long, Belle would tell me, "If you don't feel like talking, Samuel, that's all right, but my momma always said that silence invites the eternal rest, know what I'm saying? So I'm gonna fill up the air with words." And then she would start into a long story about her family or August's family or old times.

In between, she tried to get me to talk about going on to Canada. "What is the first thing you gonna do when you get up there to freedom, Samuel?" she would ask as she wrung out another cloth for Harrison's forehead. "You thinking about how it will be up there in Canaday? What it'll be like to be free your whole life?"

I tried to think about freedom, but the only thing I could see in my mind was a big, empty field. And the free people wandering around in that field were holding nothing in their hands. If you were free of everything, what did you have left? That's what I kept on thinking. Freedom was just like being given a cornfield in winter, with everything green pulled up and taken away.

Even my momma was nothing but a shadow in that field. Only thing I could see was a far-off wagon with her sitting inside it, the same as Lilly said she looked like when she left.

"Don't you want to be free?" Belle would ask, giving me a strange look. "Don't you want to get away from your mean master for good?"

"Yes'm." I nodded, trying to be polite.

Belle said that I would get up to Canada and I would be free to work the same as August worked every day, and I would get paid money for my hard work.

August worked on something called the cars. "Not carts," he said. "Cars." Every morning before sunup, he walked to the white town of Hillsboro with two other colored men from the Hollow. Sometimes I watched him leave. But it always seemed strange to me that no whitefolks followed behind him. He just puffed on his pipe, swung his lantern back and forth, and walked into the morning darkness. No whitefolks around at all.

One evening, August took me to see the cars he worked on. Harrison was restless, and Belle said I needed to look at something besides his suffering, day after day. "You been sitting by his bed, day and night, for almost a week now," she said. "Go on with August and look at something else."

So we cut through a wheat field that August said divided the Hollow from the start of the town of Hillsboro. It was getting dark, and August said we would have to hurry back.

As we came out of a small woods, I heard a low rumble. Sounded like far-off thunder, although there were no clouds above our heads at all. The only thing in the sky was the setting sun. As I looked up, a shiver went through me. How could thunder come from an empty sky?

The rumble grew louder.

My eyes darted back toward the woods we'd just walked through. "You hear something?" I said to August, trying to keep my voice as calm as water.

But August just leaned his head back and laughed. "You

never heard the sound of an iron horse before?" he chuckled. "You in for a real su-prise."

My heart pounded.

Lilly used to say that the Devil thundered through the sky at night on his big horse, looking for people's souls to steal away. "Just like that," she would snap her fingers. "You do something bad, you sittin on the Devil's horse. Gone."

"There," August said. "Look."

I pulled in all my breath.

Coming across the field in front of us was an enormous black cookstove, big as a house. Black smoke poured from its wide chimney. Parts and wheels on the side of the cookstove moved without any hands touching them, and a loud bell clanged back and forth by itself.

August shouted to be heard over the thunder. "Nothing to be scared of, right? Ain't this something to see?"

Behind the stove came a whole line of houses and sheds, flying on wheels. August pointed and hollered that those were the cars he loaded everyday. I could see whitefolks' faces inside some of the rolling cars and my heart thudded. What would happen to those poor people? What had they done wrong?

And then the iron horse was gone.

Around us, the fields grew silent. August swatted at a cloud of white flies and squinted over at me. "You scared by that?" He grinned and smacked his big hand on my shoulder. "You scared. I can tell." He waved at the place where the horse had been.

"Nothing but a railroad. Same as riding in a wagon, only it runs with smoke and fire 'stead of horses."

Never heard of those kinds of wagons before. I tried to conjure up a picture of what kind of person would be foolish enough to ride in a wagon that ran on fire. Cassius Hackler maybe. He took the horses sometimes and rode them near to death.

August paused and looked at me. "Runaways, they hide on the cars all the time and take them north. After I sneak you into Hillsboro at night, and slip you onto one of them railroad cars, you gonna be free and clear in no time. Can't travel no faster than that."

I stared at August.

"You sayin me and Harrison gonna ride that way?"

"Well, now," August said. He stooped over and pulled up a field-grass stem. "Might be. Could be." He stuck the grass stem in his mouth and chewed slowly. "Or might be you gonna have to go by your ownself first. Might be we can send Harrison by the cars later, how 'bout that?"

"Ain't goin north without Harrison," I said over my shoulder. I started back toward the Hollow, as if August might be thinking of putting me on the railroad right then. "He gets well, we gonna keep walkin to Canaday. We got things all figured out."

But when we got back to the house, Belle was waiting for us at the door. She held a melted-down candle in her hand and curls of brown hair stuck out from under her white cap.

"Harrison's been out of his senses," she said in a tight voice. "I didn't know when you were coming back, and he's been going on and on something terrible."

I flew past August and Belle, up the small stairs.

Harrison was lying in the bed, but his hands twisted and untwisted the quilt that covered him, as if he was trying to wring the stars right out of it. "That you?" he said, his eyes staring strange at me, as if he didn't know who I was. Running his tongue across his lips, which were split from fever, he whispered something.

I leaned closer. "What, Harrison?"

"Where's Belle?" he said slowly, looking around.

Belle and August were standing in the doorway, but Belle shook her head. "Don't matter what you tell him, he's not asking for me, he's wanting to talk to somebody else named Belle."

"Belle and August Henry is taking care of you," I tried to tell Harrison. "You been sick with the lung fever."

But he just glared at me.

"I ain't sick," he snapped. "I'm askin for Belle, you hear? Now, you tell me where Belle's gone to. Where they taken her?"

I tried to remember all the gone folks that Lilly used to talk about when we were working—her children, and the field hands that came through, and the slaves that used to work for Old Mas Hackler. I thought about the stones and markers in the little Negro burying-ground and Lilly pointing to each one and telling me who was who. But I didn't remember anyone being called Belle.

"I don't know nobody named Belle," I told him. "Who you talking about?"

Harrison's eyes darted nervously around the room. "My wife, Belle," he whispered. "We run away and was caught a few days ago. Ain't you heard? Me and Belle and the baby was caught in the hayloft when the baby started up cryin.'"

I remembered how Harrison had talked about being caught in a hayloft when we were hiding in the woods. He had gone out of his senses when I had gotten us lost, and he started worrying about being caught. Had he talked about a woman named Belle then too?

Harrison reached over and curled his fingers around my shirtsleeve. "Where'd they go and take Belle? Tell me, child." He stared at me, wild-eyed. "Tell me where they took her and the baby."

"There, now. You got to settle down," Belle Henry said, coming over and pushing Harrison's shoulders back to the pillow. "Who's the baby you talking about? What's her name?"

Harrison leaned back against the pillow and closed his eyes. "Hannah," he breathed. "My baby girl's name is Hannah."

I felt myself spinning and falling through a red-star sky.
Hannah was my momma's name.

"Don't keep trying to make heads or tails of the things he's saying, Samuel," August said. "He's all mixed up with the fever. Just come on downstairs and leave him to rest a while."

And if my momma was one of Harrison's children . . .

"When he gets out of that fever and comes back to his right senses, you can sit down, talk all you want. Find out who Belle and the baby is then."

All the breath squeezed out of me . . .

Harrison was my granddaddy.

Harrison's Secret

That night, I sat in the chair beside Harrison's bed. Looked down at his tired, worn face, trying to find something that was the same as mine. Did he have the same eyes as mine? Or the same kind of chin? Or forehead?

But, truth is, no matter how hard I looked, I couldn't see a thing. He looked the same as always. Nothing like me.

I took the roll of gray yarn out of my pocket and thought about my momma in Canada. I wondered if I saw her, if there would be anything that was the same as me. "Gingerbread skin," Lilly always said. "She had the same kinda skinny-long bones you have and gingerbread skin."

Or maybe I wouldn't know her either.

Around me and Harrison, the room changed from evening gray to night black to the blue shadows of early morning. Sitting there, thinking, I was afraid to close my eyes. Seemed like if I did, Harrison and my momma would get up and leave me altogether. Would slip through my fingers like water and disappear.

And then, as the first sun came into the room, Harrison opened his eyes.

Just like that.

He turned his head, looked over at me, and said sharp and clear as a bell, "Where we at, Samuel?" He waved his arm toward the little window. "This Canaday?"

"BELLE! AUGUST!" I hollered.

They came running up the steps still in their nightclothes. "Oh, Lord, Lord, Lord!" I heard Belle saying to August. "What we gonna do now?" She came into the room with her hand pressed against her mouth and her hair stuck out all over her head. And August came in with his head bowed down in his palms.

You coulda knocked them both over with a feather when they saw that Harrison had his eyes open and wasn't dead.

That very same day, Harrison sat up and ate three spoonfuls of soup by himself. And the next day, he ate a whole corn cake and a bowl of stew. But I waited one more day before I asked Harrison about his wife and the baby in the hayloft. Belle Henry said I should have known better than to ask him questions, even then.

But he was sitting back against a pillow, eating a bowl of ham soup. Looked almost like his old self. And so I said real quiet, "You ever have a wife called Belle?"

That stopped the spoon right in front of his mouth, and he looked at me.

"Who tol' you that?" he said sharp.

My heart thudded, and seemed like all the words I had thought of saying dried up in my mouth. "When you had the fever, you was calling out for people and your wife, Belle," I said low, keeping my eyes down. "Only, I didn't know you had a wife called Belle."

"You ain't s'posed to know, that's why." Harrison glared at me. "Ain't no secrets no more, I guess." He circled his spoon around and around the bowl, fast.

"Well, I does know," I kept on.

Harrison sighed loud. "My wife, Belle, she worked in the kitchen with Lilly," he said. "Years and years ago. Way before you was born."

"Someone took her away?"

Harrison looked hard at me. "You want to know what happened to Belle?" he said. "She was lost in a card game. Old Mas Hackler, he come into the kitchen one night and told her, 'Belle, you belong to Master West now. He won you in the game of cards we were playing, fair and square, and he's gonna take you with him tomorrow. To Virginia.' "

Harrison stared over at the window. "That night, me and Belle run off."

His voice got quiet. "That was a long, long time ago. We hid in that same tree you and me sat in. And the next day, we run to the hayloft of an old barn. And that's where we got caught. In that hayloft."

"That when they took Belle away?"

Harrison closed his eyes and nodded. "Old Mas Hackler, he brought me home and beat me 'til even Lilly figured I would die. And the other master took Belle away, and I never set eyes on her again, never heard of her again and—" Harrison's eyes snapped open. "So that's who my wife, Belle, was," he said sharp.

"Long, long time ago. Now, I ain't talkin about that old past no more. Take this bowl downstairs." He smacked the soup bowl on the bed table and waved his hand toward the door. " 'Fore the room is full of flies."

Downstairs, I could hear August and Belle talking, and the rhythmic thump of the spinning wheel. Truth is, I shouldn't have said another word. But just before I walked down the stairs, I turned around and said quick, "Was there a baby when you run off, too?"

Harrison leaned forward and fixed his eyes on me. "I didn't say nothin about a baby," he whispered, his eyes crackling fire. "Did I?"

I looked down at that empty soup bowl, not daring to say another word.

"Know how MANY I lost in my life, Samuel?" Harrison hissed. "I lost as many people as there is stars on this quilt." Poking a finger at each star, he recited names I'd never heard before. "Mary Epps, my birth momma. Sold. My father, James Johnson. Whipped to death. Emeline and Rebecca, my two little sisters. One sold. One sent off as a wedding gift. My three brothers, Abraham, Charles, and James . . ." He jabbed a finger at three stars. "All put in irons and sold south, same time they sold me north to Old Mas Hackler."

He crumpled the corner of the quilt in his hands. "And my only wife, Belle, worth more than all the stars in the sky—took away from me and never heard from again."

He raised a trembling finger and pointed at me. "I don't know what you heard, Samuel, but I ain't answering no more of your questions. It's better to be all alone in this world, you just remember that. You can't lose nothin then. After your momma was sold, I told Lilly that the Lord Almighty could strike me down, but I was gonna raise you as if you was all alone in this world. 'Maybe someday if we git free, maybe I'll tell him then,' I said."

I knew it sure as anything. Harrison was my granddaddy.

"Why you standing there, staring at me?" he snapped. "Go on downstairs and leave me be." Then he closed his eyes, folded his arms across his chest, and wouldn't say another word.

Didn't matter, though. Word went around the Negro Hollow that snow was on its way that night, and there was no more time for talking anyhow.

Snow Coming

"Snow?" Harrison said, sitting up fast when August told us.

But August said the snow wasn't coming from the sky. It was riding up from the South. On whitefolks' horses. August said he'd heard in town that some whitefolks would knock on all the doors of the Hollow that night and sift through the cracks. If you didn't want to be caught, you had better be ready with your free papers. Or take to your heels and run before they got there.

"They after us?" Harrison asked sharp, and I thought about Master Hackler and Cassius still looking for us more than two weeks after we had gone. There'd be no kind of punishment terrible enough to meet the trouble of that. Not if they caught us.

August shook his head. "Could be after anybody. Could be a master tracking down his runaways, or patrols rounding up what they can find, or one of the constables from town just nosing round. All we know is they got white skin."

Me and Harrison didn't have any choice but to run. "Gotta put you on the railroad tonight," August said. "Nothin more me and Belle can do."

In the kitchen, Belle put together a sack of food for us. While Harrison got ready, I stood by the table and watched her hands fly, folding a piece of cloth around a turnover pie and a half-dozen biscuits. "You just take care, Samuel, you hear?" she said, keeping her head down. "You just keep your eyes open and help Harrison along the way, as much as you can."

I thought about how Belle had stayed up with me night after night, soaking cloths for Harrison's head and fixing brandy and egg, trying to keep him from dying of the lung fever. Had we gone and brought them trouble too?

"Something gonna happen to you?" I asked. "From the whitefolks?"

Belle shook her head. "Me and August and the rest of the colored folks just lay low. Mind our business. Could be they cause a little trouble—trample some of our gardens or steal something—but we own our free papers, so they can't take us nowhere we don't want to go."

Maybe if me and Harrison got free papers, we could come back and live in the Hollow. That's what my mind said. Bring my momma and Lilly too. And if Master Hackler came looking for us, we could just hold up those papers like they were some kind of powerful big wall between us and him.

"You ready?" August came into the kitchen and lifted the old pistol out of the clay pot by the door. "Don't have no time to waste."

Belle leaned over and gave me a quick hug, her hands dusting my shoulders with flour. "Good-bye, Samuel," she whispered. "Watch your step, now."

My mind felt stuck. Seemed like the words I thought of

saying were too small and what I wanted to tell August and Belle was too big. I looked down at my feet. "Yes'm, thank you," was all that came whispering out of my mouth.

Harrison waited for us outside. He was leaning on his walking stick and staring out into the night. Seemed strange to see him standing there on the steps, same as when we first came to the Hollow. "You hear something?" August said as he pulled the door shut.

"Maybe," Harrison whispered. "Let's git a-movin."

The night air was warm and still, and it smelled like a smokehouse was going somewhere. Over our heads, the moon was already bright in the sky. I squinted up at it.

Too bright, I thought.

As we crept through patches of moonlight, I felt as if the world was holding a bunch of candles right over our heads. Harrison was breathing loud and coughing, and August kept taking quick looks behind us, putting his finger to his lips to be quiet so he could listen for something coming.

Suddenly, there was the sound of fast hoofbeats behind us.

Me and August dove face-flat in the short grass, and Harrison hunched down and pressed his face into his coat, trying to cover up the sound of his coughing. My heart pounded in my ears. Anyone coming by would see us. We were caught out in the open.

Three horses passed by, close enough for us to hear the

sound of their hard breathing. "Gid-up, girl, gid-up, gid-up!" The riders were laughing loud and shouting to their horses.

I didn't dare lift my head to see if I knew any of those riders. Even after they passed us, I stayed stuck to the ground. Seemed like the sound of their voices echoed in the air, even after they had long gone.

A shiver went through me. Were they the snow that was coming?

"Railroad's down this road," August whispered and pointed. "Just a little ways more."

The iron horse sat next to a cluster of dark buildings, but no wheels were turning or smoke coming out of it this time. Looked like it was sleeping almost. Beyond the buildings, I could see the lights of the white town of Hillsboro.

"You gonna be riding in the whiskey car," August whispered. He waved his hand in the direction of the cars. "Dark as pitch inside. But all you does is hide in there, back of the whiskey barrels, keep quiet, and come morning, that railroad is gonna take you all the ways to the lake."

Harrison was quiet for a while, like he was thinking.

"What lake we talkin about?" he said.

August looked over at Harrison and shook his head back and forth, grinning a little. "The one with Canaday on the other side of it, I imagine."

"How we s'posed to know THAT," Harrison asked,

pointing his walking stick at the railroad, "if me and Samuel is shut inside the car?"

"Well, now." August cleared his throat. "I ain't been on the cars my ownself, but folks say you just stay on them until they don't go no further. And when they don't go no further, then you know you come to the lake." He squinted at Harrison. "I figure it's prob'ly gonna take you all day with the cars stopping and starting the way they do. After dark, they say a white fellow at the lake opens all the cars and whistles."

"Whistles?" Harrison said.

"Some kinda little tune. That's what I been tol'. And you s'posed to whistle back, and when he hears that, he takes folks to the boats."

Harrison didn't say a word, just shook his head slowly from side to side.

"We never had no one come back here to the Hollow, so they must get to Canaday, I figure," August said, looking down and kicking the dirt with his shoe. "You ready, then? Better get on the car while everything's good and quiet." He stood up and took a quick look around. "Stay close, you hear?"

But I didn't want to get on those railroad cars. Nohow. Harrison hadn't seen them thundering across the field, but I had.

"Lord Almighty," Harrison whispered as we crept closer to the railroad. "Ain't seen nothin like this my whole life."

August pushed open the door of one of the cars, and the sour-sweet smell of whiskey drifted out. There were no windows like the other cars I'd seen with whitefolks inside. August said it was a freight-carrying car. It carried things, not people.

"You want me to help you climb in?" he said to Harrison.

But Harrison sat on the edge of the car and slid his own legs inside, one at a time, and I crawled in behind him. It was dark inside that car. Couldn't even see where Harrison had gone to at first. Nothing but kettle black in front of me.

Outside, August whispered good-bye.

Harrison leaned out the door and said low, "Me and Samuel's always gonna be in your debt for what you done for us. Ain't no two ways 'bout it."

"Naw," August answered, waving his hand. "That's what we does. You move on to Canaday, now, and don't pay us no more thought. Just keep yo'selves hid, remember."

But my heart leaped as the door slid closed and the latch fell into place. Seemed like everything suddenly vanished in darkness. August and Belle were gone. The Negro Hollow was gone. The field, the night sky—everything gone.

"Harrison!" I whispered loud.

But somebody else answered me.

"Who's there?" a voice said from inside the car.

Ordee Lee

"That you, Samuel?" Harrison said sharply.

"No," a colored man's voice said with a low chuckle. "I ain't Samuel."

"Samuel," Harrison hissed. In the darkness, his hand wrapped around my arm and pulled me back toward the door we had come through. "Who's hidin in this car with us?" he called out. "Somebody else in here?"

"You runaways?" the voice echoed.

"You tell us who you is first," Harrison snapped. He took another step backward, until our shirt cloth was up against the latched door of the car. Nowhere else to go. We were shut inside the four walls of the whiskey car.

"We got a gun and knife with us, you hear?" Harrison called out, even though we didn't have a thing except Belle's biscuits and turnover pie in our hands. And I had a little roll of yarn with the words *Chat-ham Canaday* in my pocket. "So you better not give us no trouble."

There was quiet. I could hear the other fellow breathing and sniffling loud and clearing his throat. "I sho' didn't run all the ways from Kentucky to get shot at and kilt. Not by two folks the same color as me. Who you think you are, anyways?" There was the smell of a candle being lit and then the sound of shoes shuffling around the barrels. "Lemme see what you look like."

The fellow that came toward us was just about the tallest black fellow I had ever seen. It looked as if someone had taken his body and stretched it in the middle, like it was a piece of dough, and then taken his arms and legs and pulled on them too. Never seen such long arms and legs on anybody before.

"You the ones I been talkin to?" he said, shuffling over. Holding up his flickering stub of a candle, he leaned closer. His eyes were big and set far apart, and they stared, checking us over real serious. First Harrison, then me.

Then the man's whole face cracked into a crooked grin. "Why, you both runaways too, ain't you?" He shook a finger at Harrison. "You only funnin with me. Here I thought you was planning to grind my bones to powder, the way you was sounding . . ."

"You just go on back where you was and leave us be," Harrison snapped.

But the fellow didn't pay Harrison any mind and kept right on talking loud. "You the first runaways I come across. I'm Ordee Lee, belonged to Master Webster from Maysville, Kentucky. I run off last week, and I been hopping one car after another trying to get north." He tapped the wall behind us with his knuckles. "You know where we is? We close to Canaday? You know anything about how to get up there?"

"Hush, now," Harrison said sharply. "Folks outside is gonna hear you."

The man reached into his worn-out coat. "Want to see my

family? I got a beautiful family back in Kentucky, where I come from." Pulling out a folded-up piece of paper, he said, "Here they is."

He handed his candle to Harrison and opened the paper in his hand carefully, square by square, until he held the whole piece open, and I could see what was inside.

I had to swallow hard when I saw it.

Three knots of blackfolks' hair lay on that white paper. Looked like it was a page from a letter or book, folded and folded. And in the middle of all those fancy words, the blackfolks' hair lay there like three lost rings.

"This my wife, Nancy," Ordee Lee said, pointing to the darkest ring. "Most pretty woman in the world. And these our babies, Isaiah and little Moses." Softly, he traced his finger around the two smallest rings. "Moses, he just born in the spring, got lungs like two bellows, and Isaiah, he just walkin when I went to my master and—"

Ordee Lee's voice caught and stopped. He looked at us, his eyes blinking fast.

"When you went to your master and did what?" Harrison said, holding up Ordee Lee's candle and squinting at him.

Ordee Lee folded up the piece of paper without saying a word and stuck it into his coat. Then he cast his eyes quick around the car and over his shoulder, like he was expecting something to come out of the shadows.

"When you what?" Harrison said again.

Ordee Lee cracked all of his knuckles and twisted his hands together. "When I brought a shovel down on his head," he whispered. "And tried to kill him."

"What?" Harrison stared, and I could feel all the blood drain right down to my feet. Ordee Lee had gone after his own master. He had taken a shovel to a white man. There was no trouble worse than that.

Ordee Lee's hands knotted and unknotted themselves. "I took a shovel and hit him. Run, they says. Run. I run all night. Never looked back. Just run." He reached in his coat for the folded-up paper again and held it toward us. "He was gonna sell me off from them. My Nancy and Isaiah and Moses," he said, tapping the paper. "Why would somebody do something like that? That's what I kept on sayin. Why?"

Ordee Lee's voice trembled. "The day they was planning to take me away from them, I just raised the shovel, raised it, and brought it—" Ordee Lee took a step backward, staring wide-eyed at us. "I'm gonna go back to my own side of the car and lie down," he said fast. "Do 'preciate meetin you." And he shuffled into the darkness, bumping and stumbling into barrels, leaving his candle behind.

Harrison stared at the flickering candle in his hands. White wax dripped all over his fingers and onto the floor. "We been stuck inside a car full of whiskey and trouble, Samuel." He shook his head. "Snow outside and trouble inside."

All night, me and Harrison sat inside that car, waiting. Then morning came, and the car started to move. I was sleeping on the floor when I caught the sharp smell of burning wood. I lifted up my head, looking around for Harrison in the gray shadows. Outside, there was a loud bell ringing and someone's voice calling out.

"Harrison," I said, sitting up fast. "Something wrong?"

Harrison was over by the wall of the car with his eyes pressed against the chinks in the wood, trying to see out. "Can't see nothin," he whispered, turning around, his eyes wide with fear. "Only thing I smell is smoke—"

The car jolted forward and back, all of a sudden. Harrison tried to reach for the side of the car and fell against a stack of barrels. He groaned and put his forehead down in his hands.

"ORDEE LEE!" I hollered.

As the car began to sway and rumble forward, Ordee Lee came flying out of the shadows in the back of the car, going from one barrel to another, holding on. "You callin for me?" he said, looking around wide-eyed. "Something done happen while I was sleepin?"

Harrison was on his hands and knees trying to get himself up. "Ain't you never been on a railroad before?" Ordee Lee hollered over the noise. "You gotta hold on to something. Here—" He reached for Harrison. "You just take ahold of my arm—"

Me and Ordee Lee pulled Harrison to standing. Around

us, the car swayed and shook like thunder, going faster and faster. Whiskey sloshed back and forth in the barrels. My heart roared in my ears.

"We on fire?" Harrison hollered.

"Naw." Ordee Lee shook his head and waved his hand at the front of the car. "They's burning wood up there in that iron horse and making clouds full of smoke and soot. Come afternoon, you gonna be tasting them ashes in your mouth, believe me."

Harrison looked toward the door of the car. Light flashed through the chinks in the walls, on and off, making thin stripes of lightning on our faces. Felt like we were heading straight to the gates of hell itself.

"How fast we going, you think?" Harrison asked.

"Fast," Ordee Lee hollered. "No old horse and wagon'd keep up with us, that's for sure. Not 'less it had wings."

Going North

All day, the whiskey car stopped and started at places we couldn't see. More places than we could count, just like August had said. We heard people walking past the car, and barrels being rolled and loaded. Me and Harrison and Ordee Lee stayed crouched down in the back of the car each time we stopped, in case someone opened the door. But no one did.

When we were moving, Ordee Lee almost wore out the floor. Pacing back and forth, he talked and cracked his knuckles and tapped his fingers on each of the barrels. He told us about all the cars he had been on since running off. A pork-barrel car. A lumber car. A baggage car. And this one.

Didn't breathe a word again about his master or what he had done.

"Trouble is," he said, "you don't know the direction the cars is going when you get on. So one went west instead of north. Another went south, and took me all the way back to Cincinnati—prob'ly woulda took me to the fields to pick cotton," he chuckled, "if I hadn't been watchin close. And another just sat on the tracks, never moved once."

"This one's going north to the lake," Harrison told him. "That's what we heard in Hillsboro."

"Huh," Ordee Lee said, chewing on a piece of straw. "We'll see 'bout that. Maybe we open the door and it's New Ore-leans."

Harrison said that the cotton fields of the south were dead hot, and if we were going south, the car would be getting hotter and hotter inside, and we would know it. The wind coming through the chinks in the car was cool—cold almost—when we were moving, and it smelled like pastures and fields outside. So Harrison said he was sure we were heading the right direction. North.

But Ordee Lee kept on worrying and walking all day. "Thought you says someone was going to come for us and let us out? When they s'posed to come?" he would ask Harrison for the hundredth time. "We been on this railroad car all day, where's that lake gone to?"

Didn't matter how many times Harrison told him that we had to wait until dark. Each time the car came to another stop, Ordee Lee would ask, "You think we come to the lake yet? You think Canaday's out there now?"

Me and Harrison kept to our own side of the car. Sitting there in the rumbling darkness, I tried to think about Canada. Tried to conjure up a picture of people waiting there for us, the way people wait for visitors.

"What you think it's gonna be like?" I asked Harrison. But Harrison closed his eyes and said it was bad luck to talk about things before they happened.

I remembered Young Mas Seth showing me a silver coin once and telling me that I had to chase him all over, trying to take it away. Seemed like Canada was the same as that silver coin. We had chased all over, and now we had almost caught it.

I tried to picture what Canada would look like. Tried to picture myself living in a real house and walking around calling Harrison my granddaddy. Or maybe we would live in Chat-ham with my momma if she had a spare bedchamber. And maybe if I was free, I could get up some mornings and do what I wanted to, just like Young Mas Seth. I could carry one or two fancy white-folks' books in my hands, and have a mule to ride, and learn to write words like Mr. Keepheart.

Strange to think about all of that. It made me feel scared and pleased inside at the same time.

"Car's slowin down," Ordee Lee whispered loud. "Listen."

The rumbling deepened and lengthened like a horse in a slow gallop. After a string of jolts and pulls, we came to a stop. Only this time, we didn't move on again. The bell stayed silent, and one by one, all the voices outside died away.

Seemed like an hour passed, maybe more. It was night out-side, we could tell, because the car was pitch-black inside. We heard an owl hooting and a pair of tomcats fighting and clawing. "If this ain't the height of madness," Ordee Lee said, lying down next to us and flinging his arms over his face. "They ain't gonna let us out. We gonna shrivel up and die locked in this here rail-road."

Harrison didn't say a word. His rigor mortis had set in, bad, from being on the hard floor all day. He was leaning against one wall, with his head down on his chest. I could hear him whispering the words of the same song, over and over. "Lord, Lord, Lord," he mumbled low. "What you want me to stay here for, this ol' world ain't a friend no more, no friend, no more, what you want me to stay here for . . ."

And then there was the soft sound of footsteps coming around the car.

My heart thudded.

The latch on our car moved, rattled, and the door creaked a little ways open. I could hear the sound of someone leaning in. Breathing.

"Tu-ee. Tu-ee," the person whistled real low. It sounded just like a little night bird whistling. But before me and Harrison could whistle back, Ordee Lee jumped up and said loudly, "We here. Don't go and shut that door. There's three of us colored folks hidin in here."

"Lord Almighty," Harrison hissed. "You hush, now."

It didn't matter because whoever was outside had already heard us.

There was a long silence, as if they were waiting, or listening, or maybe thinking about shutting the door and leaving us right there. "You runaways?" a hoarse voice said finally. Sounded like a white voice.

We didn't have a single choice but to answer.

"Yes." Harrison heaved a sigh. "We is."

"All right," the voice said quickly. "Come out then."

Sliding our hands along the tops of the whiskey barrels, we

moved slowly through the darkness toward the door. First Ordee Lee, then me, then Harrison. I could see the night sky and a few pale wisps of clouds through the open square. There were stars out, too.

It sent a shiver clear through me.

Everything looked exactly the same as my dream in the white-folks' church.

I remembered leaning over the hole in the church floor and staring at the same stars and the night sky. I remembered how Reverend Pry and Mr. Keepheart lowered Harrison into that open square, and how he had floated away from me, spinning and turning and falling in that terrible darkness . . .

I glanced quick at the shadow of Harrison behind me. His fingers curled around my shoulder. "Keep movin," he said, pushing me forward as if he could hear what I was thinking. "Ain't nothin wrong."

But, truth is, the nearer we got to that doorway, the more I could feel something wrong. In my mind, I saw Reverend Pry and Mr. Keepheart shaking their heads and giving me that sad, sorry look—

"Go on," Harrison whispered.

My heart pounded as we climbed out of the car. Seemed like there was no ground at all, as if the three of us were just jumping down into darkness.

"That all of you?" A man stepped out of the shadows of the

railroad car. He was a white fellow, with hunched-over shoulders and short bowlegs. His voice was strange-sounding. Sharp.

"Yes," Harrison said.

The man shook his head and spit a stream of tobacco into the darkness. "Bad night to come here to Sandusky. Slave catcher's bloodhounds got loose and killed twenty-four sheep outside of town two nights ago. You hear about that?"

"What?" Ordee Lee stared wide-eyed at the man. "Ain't this the North?"

I shot a quick look at Harrison, not understanding at all how slave catchers and dogs could be after us. Not when we had come all this way. We had taken railroads fast as the wind. How could bloodhounds still be after us here?

The man chuckled real low. "You figured everything in the North was free and clear, huh?" he said, shaking his head back and forth. "Well, now, I'm purely sorry to tell you poor folks that you are in more danger here"—he waved his hand at the darkness—"than probably anywhere else you run from."

He looked at us. Me, Harrison, and Ordee Lee stood next to the whiskey car, like we had been struck dumb by lightning.

"See," the white fellow kept on, "the lake's the last place they can pounce on you and take you back to the folks who own you, that's why. And there's always a bunch of man-hunters who watch our boats and make a living doing just that."

He pushed the door of the whiskey car closed. "Don't

know what else woulda killed those poor sheep, if it wasn't some slave catcher's bloodhounds. I ain't seen the bloodhounds myself, that's just what I heard in town," he said. "But the other boys on the boat told me not to come here tonight. They said I was gonna get myself caught with runaways or torn up by dogs, and I should just leave the colored folks alone."

The man spit into the darkness. "But I ain't afraid of nothing. That's what I told them. See if Ol' Bowlegs doesn't smuggle a few coloreds on board in the morning, I said." He gave a crooked grin. "I already got thirty-one of you folks to my name this year.

"You just follow me to the docks," he said, waving his arm for us to follow. "Ain't nothing to fear."

Me, Harrison, and Ordee Lee walked behind the man like three trembly shadows, not saying a word to each other, just hurrying from one stopping place to the next. All around us were rows of dark sheds, and the air smelled strange and heavy with fish.

Ordee Lee stopped suddenly.

"You hear that?" he whispered, staring at us wide-eyed. Me and Harrison didn't wait to see what Ordee Lee was looking at in the darkness. We just jumped into the shadows of one of the buildings and crouched against a wall.

Then the sound started up again. It was a terrible creaking sound. Like a hundred old doors opening and closing. Or the rattling sound of a haunt's old bones.

My neck prickled with gooseflesh.

"Why'd you stop?" The white fellow came over to where we were hiding and looked down at us. "You want to have them bloodhounds find us?" he hissed.

Ordee Lee said he wasn't about to go anywhere with that sound.

"Ain't you never heard wood boats creaking before? That's the sound they make." The man spat. He took ahold of Ordee Lee's big arm and pointed up at the sky. "We got an hour or two before first cock crow. I can't sneak you on the boats 'til it's light. You just follow me, like I told you. Don't give me any more reason to stop."

He hurried down a dirt path between two of the buildings and ducked into an open doorway. "Gonna hide in here," he whispered.

The building smelled of rotted food. As we squinted into the darkness, I could see there were stacks of wood crates, barrels, piles of stove wood—and some things that moved. All around us, small shadows ran along the walls. My heart thudded.

Rats.

But the man didn't pay any mind to the rats crawling around him. Perching on the top of a barrel, he reached into his coat and pulled out a bottle of whiskey. "You never set foot on a big boat before?" he said, taking a long swallow and wiping his hand across his mouth. "You never saw the Mississippi?"

Me and Harrison just stood where we were, not saying a word. Seemed as if I could feel those rats running up and down my skin.

"I come from Kentucky," Ordee Lee said loudly. "Took a little skiff across the Ohio River. But I didn't like all that water floating around me. No, sir. Long time before Ordee Lee crosses a river like that again, long, long time." He paced back and forth, making little squares as he walked.

"Well, you better get used to seeing some water again," the man chuckled. "That lake you are gonna cross could swallow a hundred Ohio Rivers and prob'ly still drink up a few more." Leaning his head back, he took a loud gulp of whiskey. "When the land disappears, it'll prob'ly look like the At-land-tic Ocean to you."

Ordee Lee stopped. "What? Where's the land go?" he asked sharp.

"Where do you think?" The man wagged his head back and forth as if Ordee Lee was as thick as turnips. "You leave the land here behind and you don't see any more land until you get to Canada."

My breath caught in my chest. I remembered how Lilly always said, "When we go on to the Promised Land someday, Samuel, we is gonna leave this old, tough world behind and not see any more land until we get up there in the clouds."

"How far off is Canaday?" Ordee Lee asked, knotting and unknotting his fingers. "How long we stay on them boats?"

"Be there by evening with a strong wind," the man said as he took another swallow of whiskey. "Long after nightfall if it's calm."

"Lord," I heard Harrison say under his breath. "Let those winds be strong."

Through the open door of the shed, the sky grew lighter and lighter, like a piece of dark dye cloth being washed. It was getting close to morning. All around us, there was the sound of wagons creaking down the mud roads between the buildings. Barrels rolled past the doorway, and people talked in sharp, northern-sounding voices outside.

But, truth is, the closer we got to the break of day, the more my heart pounded. *Trouble, trouble, trouble.*

Harrison cleared his throat and pointed at the door. "It time?" he said loudly to the man.

The man rubbed his eyes and pushed his hat back on his head like he had been sleeping. "Well, now, could be. But I done this trick a hundred times, you know," he said slowly, his words all running together. "All you does is just roll a few of these flour barrels"—he patted the side of the barrel he was sitting on—"to the *Otter,* the same as the other colored folks loading cargo, and you are as good as free. Nobody is gonna stop you for working on the docks. I done this trick a hundred times. A hundred and one times." He put a finger to his lips. "Shhh. Just keep hid," he said, grinning at Harrison. "Ol' Bowlegs will have his little look-around." Tucking the whiskey bottle in his coat, he staggered slow and swaying through the open door.

After he was gone, Ordee Lee whispered, "You think the three of us gonna be free today, huh? You think we gonna get to Canaday today?" He drummed his fingers on the top of a wood barrel. "You think these barrels gonna get us to FREE-dom? You think that fellow was tellin us the truth?"

"You hush," Harrison snapped. " 'Fore people out there hear you."

The man stuck his head through the doorway. "Roll those flour barrels right out here," he said loudly. "Looks fine and clear. Let's load up the cargo, fellows."

But I had a strange feeling as Ordee Lee turned two barrels on their sides for us to push toward the door. Me and Harrison set our hands down, side by side, on one barrel. Ordee Lee took the other.

Looking down at our brown hands on those flour barrels, I felt my throat tighten, squeezing tighter and tighter. *Hush,* a voice whispered in my mind. *Hush, someone's coming . . .*

"Don't have all day," the man said, waving. "Come on."

Following the man's back, we pushed our barrels out the doorway and down the dusty road to the docks. The smell of fish and the sound of the boats creaking in the wind grew stronger. The road was full of people and carts and wagons. Seemed like we were in the middle of a river of moving things.

As our barrels rolled onto the thick wood planks of the docks, my heart jumped. *We at the dock already? We this close to freedom after all this time?* The barrels rolled hard on the uneven planks. Thunk-thunk-thunk. The sound was loud. Too loud.

I kept my eyes down. Didn't look up at all of the people passing around us. Just their shoes. Fancy cloth shoes. Old patched shoes. Greased work shoes. Boots.

The boots moved in front of us. And stopped.

Ordee Lee's feet stopped.

"Get out your papers," a hard voice said to us. "Lemme see them."

Southern-sounding voice, boot-heel hard.

Fast, Ordee Lee's feet turned and spun around. They lifted off the dock like two black birds taking flight, going to freedom all by themselves—

But not fast enough.

Another pair of boots stepped behind us, and white hands reached out and latched hard onto our arms.

If you run, the river man said, they know exactly who you are . . .

Haste Will Be Your Undoing

We were caught.

As the white hand wrapped around my arm, I felt everything inside me crumble and turn to dust. Only thing left was my skin and my eyes. Everything else gone.

All the way from Kentucky me and Harrison had run and run, with the Lord looking out for us the whole way, seemed like, and all the time, he had known we would be caught on the docks where the boats go to Canada—that's what I kept thinking. He just let us run and run, knowing we would be caught at the very end, standing on the dock to freedom.

Harrison's head dropped to his chest and his shoulders slumped over. I could hear him mumbling and whispering, "Belle . . . Belle . . . Belle . . . Belle," as they tied his hands together with a piece of rope.

"Cross your arms behind you," the man said sharp to Ordee Lee.

Listen, Ordee Lee. Listen. Listen.

"I said, 'Cross them,' boy."

There was the sound of a hand cracking across Ordee Lee's face. He crumpled to the wood-plank dock, and I heard the snap of the rope as they knotted his hands behind him.

"Lay down on the dock," they told me and Harrison. "And

keep still." They tied our feet together with one piece of rope. Same as if they were tying up cordwood.

"Hope you wasn't thinking of going somewhere." The one man leaned over us and grinned. He had a brown hat pulled low over his forehead and a chin stained yellow with tobacco.

The other man had narrow, close-together eyes. Those eyes stared at us like two pieces of hard flint. "I'm gonna hunt up the constable around here," he said. "If the darkies don't have free papers, they run off from somewhere, and we'll just hand them over to the jail 'til we find out where." He poked his boot toe at Ordee Lee's leg. "You watch, Crane," he said. "This one'll be worth some money."

The white birds cried overhead, and the boats creaked and sighed at the docks. People walked past us slow, like we were something to look at. I could hear voices talking all around us. Strange to say, some of the voices sounded sorry. "A pity," I thought I heard. "What a pity."

Lying on the dock, I stared up at the gulls, wheeling and circling over our heads. I thought about Lilly and all the trouble she had seen, and Harrison being caught and beaten for running off, and his wife, Belle, being lost forever in a card game. I thought about my momma being caught when she was a baby, and then being sold off and taken away after I was born . . .

Seemed like all of the blackfolks were standing in a long, long line in my mind. Waiting for me to meet trouble, same as them. *Our hard times is almost over,* they whispered, *but your hard times is all ahead of you.*

The man who had caught us paced back and forth, and told people to move on and mind their business. "Don't you have nothing better to look at?" he would snap. "Go on with what you were doing."

Closing my eyes, I pictured me and Harrison turning ourselves into some of the white birds in the sky and flying away to freedom. I pictured the people on the docks gathering around. Everyone watching us lift from the dock and fly away to Canada, just like a pair of white paper birds . . .

And then, out of the clear blue sky, a small thought came to me.

My eyes flew open. I turned my head to look over at Ordee Lee. He was lying next to me, his whole face twisted up with crying and tears. "Ordee Lee," I whispered.

The boots shuffled farther off, looking at something, not noticing.

"Ordee Lee!" I hissed.

But Ordee Lee wouldn't answer.

Plan a way out, the river man had said. Haste will be your undoing.

Heels echoed loud on the dock, coming closer. The sharp-eyed man had brought the constable, a big man with black hair and earlocks down to his chin almost. Smelled strong of onions when he leaned toward us.

"Let them sit up," the constable said, leaning over and frowning at us. "They ain't sheep." I watched his eyes, the way they looked at me and Harrison and Ordee Lee lying there with our feet tied together and our hands behind us. And I saw something in his eyes. Maybe.

"They can get themselves up." The man called Crane laughed and spit.

"I ain't movin'," Harrison whispered, turning his head to look away. "Go on and shoot me right here."

"All three of them are somebody's slaves," the man with the sharp eyes said loud. "I know three runaway slaves when I see them. Probably one thousand dollars sitting right there."

I knew dirt when I saw it too. The two men who had caught us were dirt. That's what I said in my mind.

The constable heaved a sigh and tapped one of the loose planks with his boot. There were people circled around us now, I could tell, and they were all quiet. Seemed like even the air was holding its breath, waiting.

"Sure they ain't got free papers put away somewhere?" the constable said slowly, clearing his throat. "You asked them?"

"They got nothing but their black skin," the man called Crane snorted. "And it ain't free. Anybody with eyes can see that."

The constable sighed again and looked down at us,

frowning. "Well, now," he said. "Hmm. Well." I saw the same thing I had seen before in his eyes. A flicker of something.

Look for weakness and plan a way out, the river man had said.

I tried my one thought. Cast it up into the sky. Just to see what would happen. "We got free papers," I said. "Truth is, we been free more than a year."

The two men who had caught us laughed loud. Spit and laughed. "Listen to the boy. Listen to him go on." The people standing around started whispering and buzzing among themselves, sounded like bees. Sounded like a whole nest of bees.

The constable grew more of a frown.

"All right," he said. "Untie them and let me see the papers he's talking about."

"Ain't no papers," the sharp-eyed man snapped.

"Untie them."

They took their time untying the rope around our feet and pulled us up to sitting, mean as they could. I looked over at Ordee Lee hunched over beside me. He had his eyes closed. Blood and tears were dried all down his cheeks.

"It's in his coat," I said to the constable. "He keeps our papers folded up in his coat."

Leaning over, the constable searched through Ordee Lee's old coat himself. Pulled out a leaf of tobacco, an apple core, a half-burnt candle from the railroad, and the square of paper.

"This it?"

He held up Ordee Lee's precious paper, and Ordee Lee turned his head and fixed me with a stare mean enough to turn bones to powder. Figured I was bringing more trouble probably.

"That ain't nothin," Ordee Lee said real low. "Ain't nothin."

In my mind, I saw Green Murdock holding up those fancy willowware bowls and telling us how he had tricked an old woman into buying them. I thought about the fine smoked ham and the new tow-linen shirt that wasn't new at all.

And I looked straight at that constable and told a lie as smooth as Green Murdock himself. "Yes, sir," I said loud. "You got our free papers."

Harrison turned his head and whispered, "Hush, Samuel."

"You awful smart for being the color you are, boy," the man with the flint eyes hissed. "I hope you know who you are talking to." Looking up at him and thinking of Master Hackler, I felt the snake squeeze around my throat.

Clumsy and impatient, the constable tore the paper as he opened it.

"Just tear the whole thing to pieces," one of the men laughed. "We won't tell a soul."

Probably no one but Ordee Lee, me, and Harrison saw the three curls of hair slip out of the paper folds and drift away on the wind. Nancy, Isaiah, and Moses. A shiver went clear through me. If anyone found out he had tried to kill a white man because of them, we would all be dead.

The constable held the paper open. Just an old scrap Ordee

Lee had stolen from a book or a letter. He glanced down at it and over at me, a flicker in his eyes. The people on the dock moved closer, waiting. The whole line of blackfolks in my mind stood at a hush.

"What does it say?" the sharp-eyed man pushed. "They free or not?"

The constable folded the paper carefully, square by square, and gave it back to me. "What do you think?" he said, keeping his eyes down. "Says they're free."

Keep Your Eye on the Sun

On the same morning that we got free from the docks and rolled our flour barrels toward the *Otter,* my momma was sitting in Chatham, Canada, at her little kitchen table. "I looked up," she told me later, "and plain as day, I saw you through my kitchen window. Three boys were playing in the street, laughing and running, and one of them was you. I said to myself, *That is exactly what my Samuel looks like right now.* And that's when I knew you were coming, sure as anything. In my mind, I knew."

But we didn't know any of that.

As we got up real slow from the docks, the constable untied our hands and told us to get busy with our work, or he would find something worse for us to do. So Harrison put his hands next to mine on the flour barrel, and I could see all of his fingers trembling like leaves. And Ordee Lee set his big-knuckled hands on his flour barrel. And we started rolling those barrels down the dock.

Seemed like everyone had their eyes on us, watching. They stepped back to let us pass. "Parted like the Red Sea," Lilly would have said. The soft thump of the barrels and the white birds calling overhead filled the air around us.

Walk as if you have the perfect right to do so. You slave or free?
Free.

Then walk like it. Walk.

I put my shoulders back a little. Lifted up my head and took a quick sideways glance at everything around us. I saw the big sailboats lining the docks, one after the other. And I saw people stopping in the middle of their work to stare at us. And in the spaces in between, I saw green-blue water just like Lilly had said, water that stretched all the way to the sky.

"Flour goes on the *Otter,* over there," someone called out to us. We rolled the barrels up a long plank to a boat that was the size of a house. Maybe two houses.

"We free?" Ordee Lee whispered. "This mean we free?"

All around us, men tugged at curls of ropes and lines. The *Otter* swayed underneath our feet. Seemed like everything around us was being set free.

Me and Harrison and Ordee Lee stood where we were, not saying a word. Just stood on the deck and looked up, as if our eyes and mouths were stuck.

Over our heads, the canvas sails of the *Otter* unrolled like warm summer clouds. And if we could have seen our future unfolding in those big sails, like my momma saw the future in her mind, we would have known what was going to happen to each of us in freedom . . .

We would have known that Ordee Lee would become a blacksmith—the finest blacksmith in Chatham, Canada. He would call himself "Isaiah Moses" after his two sons. And although he would never see his family again, he would often bring us gifts of food and money—even a real horse once. "Can't ever give enough," he would say. "For what Samuel done."

When Harrison got to Canada, he would find ponds scattered like seeds through the forests and fields around Chatham. He would choose one of his own to sit beside, and he would fish, day after day, until we all took to running from him whenever he brought home another stringer of pond fish for supper. (If you ask anyone around Chatham today, they can still point you to Harrison's Pond, and it's always full of fish right down to the very bottom.)

And when I got to Chatham, I would find my own momma sitting at her kitchen table waiting for us. She would have extra places set because she knew we were coming. "Today or tomorrow, or sometime . . ." And when we walked through the door of her house, we would hear, sure as the whole town—no, the whole country of *Canaday*—heard, that Harrison was her daddy, and I was her long-lost son.

Only person we never would have in freedom was Lilly. Lilly stayed with her children in the little Negro burying-ground on Master Hackler's land. "She's never gonna leave," Harrison said. " 'Cause that's where her family is." Each year, she would send a Christmas dollar to me, wrapped in a torn-out page from her Bible, and I saved all six of them.

But, truth is, we didn't know any of these things—not about Ordee Lee, or Harrison, or my momma, or Lilly, or what was going to happen to us in freedom at all—as we stood on the deck of the *Otter* that morning. We just stared at the white sails soaring in the endless morning sun.

"Samuel," Harrison said, grinning at me. "We done it."

He waved his arms, turning and spinning in the wind.

"Whoooeeee, Samuel," he hollered and waved. "Look up. Look up at this beautiful free sky."

Samuel and Harrison's Journey, 1859

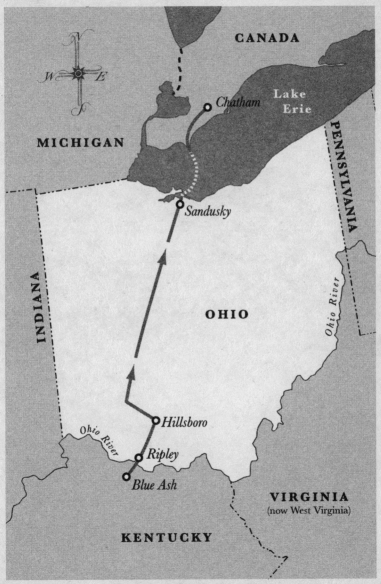

Author's Note

The Underground Railroad is a familiar American story. It is a story filled with dramatic accounts of secret rooms, brave abolitionists, and midnight journeys. But sometimes the real heroes of the story—the runaways themselves—are left in the background. What did they think and feel as they tried to reach freedom? What was their journey like? Whom did the runaways trust and whom did they fear? This book grew from my wondering about these questions. . . .

In my research, I learned that the Underground Railroad was not a clear, organized network that led runaways from the South to the North. Actually, the term referred to any safe routes or hiding places used by runaways—so there were hundreds, even thousands, of "underground railroads."

Most runaways traveled just the way that Samuel and Harrison did—using whatever temporary hiding places or means of transportation they could find. As the number of actual railroad lines increased throughout the country in the 1850s, some runaways even hid on railroad cars when traveling from one place to another. They called this "riding the steam cars" or "going the faster way."

I also discovered that runaways were not as helpless or ill prepared as they are sometimes portrayed. Historical records indicate that many slaves planned carefully for their journey. They brought provisions such as food and extra clothing with them. Since transportation and guides could cost money, some slaves saved for their escape, while others, like Samuel and Harrison, received money from individuals they met during their journey.

White abolitionists and sympathetic religious groups like the Quakers aided many runaways on the Underground Railroad. However, free African Americans played an equally important role. They kept runaways in their homes and settlements and served as guides, wagon drivers, and even decoys.

In fact, the character of the river man is based on the real-life story of a black Underground Railroad guide named John P. Parker. Like the river man, John Parker was badly beaten as a young slave, and so he never traveled anywhere without a pistol in his pocket and a knife in his belt. During a fifteen-year period, he ferried more than four hundred runaways across the Ohio River, and a $1,000 reward was once offered for his capture. After the Civil War, he became a successful businessman in Ripley, Ohio, and patented several inventions.

I am often asked whether other parts of the novel are factual. The gray yarn that is sent as a sign? The baby buried below the church floor? Lung fever? Guides named Ham and Eggs?

The answer is yes. Most of the events and names used in this novel are real, but they come from many different sources. I discovered names like Ordee Lee and Ham and Eggs in old letters and records of the Underground Railroad. The character of Hetty Scott is based on a description I found in John Parker's autobiography. The heart-wrenching tale of Ordee Lee saving the locks of hair of his family comes from a slave's actual account. However, I adapted all of this material to fit into the story of Samuel and Harrison—so time periods and locations have often been changed.

One of the most memorable aspects of writing this book was taking a trip to northern Kentucky and southern Ohio in late summer. To be able to describe the Cornfield Bottoms and the Ohio River, I walked down to the river late at night to see what it looked like and how it sounded in the darkness. To be able to write about Samuel's mother, I stood on a street corner in Old Washington, Kentucky, where slaves were once auctioned. I even stayed in houses that had been in existence during the years of the Underground Railroad.

I chose the southern Ohio and northern Kentucky region for my setting since it had been a very active area for the Underground Railroad. I selected the year 1859 because Congress passed a national law called the Fugitive Slave Act in 1850, which affected everyone involved in the Underground Railroad. Severe penalties such as heavy fines and jail time awaited anyone—white or black—who helped or harbored runaway slaves anywhere in the United States after 1850.

The law also required people to return runaway slaves to their owners, even if the runaways were living in free states like Ohio. African Americans like August and Belle, who had papers to prove their freedom, were safe from capture even though their lives were sometimes restricted by local and state "black laws." However, runaway slaves were only safe if they left the country and went to places like Canada or Mexico. That is why Samuel and Harrison had to journey all the way to Canada to be free in 1859.

So, if you visited Canada today, would you still find a peaceful place called Harrison's Pond? And is there a tumbledown farmhouse somewhere in Kentucky with an old burying-ground for slaves nearby?

Harrison's Pond and Blue Ash, Kentucky, are places in my imagination, but there are many other places to visit with solemn footsteps and remember. I hope that you will.

—Shelley Pearsall

Selected Bibliography

Coffin, Levi. *Reminiscences of Levi Coffin*. New York: Arno Press, 1968.

Lester, Julius. *To Be a Slave*. New York: Scholastic, Inc., 1968.

McCline, John. *Slavery in the Clover Bottoms: John McCline's Narrative of His Life During Slavery and the Civil War*. Edited by Jan Furman. Knoxville, Tenn.: University of Tennessee Press, 1998.

Parker, John P. *His Promised Land: The Autobiography of John P. Parker, Former Slave and Conductor on the Underground Railroad*. New York: W. W. Norton & Co., 1996.

Siebert, William H. *Mysteries of Ohio's Underground Railroad*. Columbus, Ohio: Long's College Book Company, 1951.

Still, William. *The Underground Railroad*. New York: Arno Press, 1968.

Acknowledgments

I would like to acknowledge the fellowship from the Ohio Arts Council, which provided the initial time and support to write; Jan Ridgeway and Jackie Fink, who reviewed early drafts of the manuscript; and finally, the following young readers who offered their comments throughout the writing process: Jonathan Hartman, Whitney Butler, Alexandra Zelaski, Mark Levin, Patrick and Michael Vernon, and Meaghan Igel.